THE LAST GODS

ADAM BROWNLIE

THE
LAST
GODS

THE LAST GODS
A Story of Love, New Beginners and Destiny

ISBN: 978-1-7636622-3-0   *(Hardcover)*
ISBN: 978-1-7636622-0-9   *(Paperback)*

TABLE OF CONTENTS

Chapter 1. In the Beginning....................................9

Chapter 2. Come All Ye Faithful 21

Chapter 3. The Wages of Sin Is Death 41

Chapter 4. By the Grace of God 49

Chapter 5. Until Death Do Us Part 61

Chapter 6. The End of Materialism.................... 75

Chapter 7. Why Hast Thou Forsaken Me?.................. 83

Chapter 8. The Era of Artificial Intelligence 99

Chapter 9. Thou Shalt Not Kill....................III

Chapter 10. The Era of Superintelligence 125

Chapter 11. The Era of the *Deus*....................135

Chapter 12. Nirvana Is Here....................157

Chapter 13. Life After Death 173

Chapter 14. Heaven Is Nigh 189

Epilogue.................... 195

*Some psychologists opine that part of the reason why
we stand in line for our tall Iced Caramel Macchiatos
and work our fingers to the bone to acquire the latest
sports car is to suppress, at least for a while, the nagging
little voice telling us that we're all going to die.*

—DAN GONZALEZ

CHAPTER ONE

IN THE BEGINNING

PRESENT DAY

At the intersection of East and Maple, Elodie slammed on the brakes of her Prius and groaned. She'd meant to get to church *early*, not four minutes late as Google Maps now projected.

Digging her freshly manicured nails into the soft plastic of the steering wheel, Elodie peered around the grey SUV idling in front of her. The flow of traffic streamed across East Highway with no sign of pausing. She reached over and fished her phone out of her handbag, hoping to find a podcast or something to occupy her mind. As she glanced at the screen, she noticed a new voicemail from her mother, but before she could decide whether to listen to it, a text alert popped up. For a brief, satisfying moment she thought it might be Kayla or Archer, asking if they'd see her at church—but her smile faded as she saw the message was from Markus.

Are you coming straight home after?

Elodie sighed. She'd literally just left the house. He'd made her late, and now he wanted her to rush straight home after the service?

Their argument still echoed in her head.

I get that you want us to go to church together, babe, Markus had said. *But why this one? Why this religion? What if it turns out the Catholics have it right? Then we burn in hell, despite traipsing to church every Sunday, simply because we didn't repent of our sins.*

Elodie had sighed heavily as she pulled her long blonde hair into a French twist. *Honestly, Markus, you always go to the extreme. I just think it would be nice if we were united in our beliefs.*

What you're really saying is you want us to both be Christians, Markus said, crossing his arms. He pretended he was just teasing, but she could see the annoyance reflected in his wide hazel eyes.

Why do you always have to be so difficult—

A car horn went off, startling Elodie from her thoughts. Her cheeks flushed as she glanced at the driver in the rear-view mirror; a mustachioed tough guy on a motorcycle made rude gestures in her direction. The grey SUV was already disappearing around the corner.

"Okay, asshole," she muttered through gritted teeth as she pressed down hard on the accelerator. The prius lurched forward, and she glanced down at the phone still in her hand, which now showed she was running *six* minutes late.

Out of the corner of her eye she saw a streak of movement. Then the car to her left, in the second lane, swerved into her space. With a sharp cry, Elodie jerked the steering wheel to the right.

She could almost hear her father's voice in her head. *Never overcorrect. Just hit the brakes. Better to hit an animal than a tree, or oncoming traffic.*

His warning played out like a prophecy.

Elodie watched in a strange sort of disembodied horror as her Prius lurched toward the four-lane slipstream of East Highway. Her foot caught the side of the brake, but the smooth surface of her elegant Prada heels found no purchase, sliding off the edge of the pedal. She was suddenly staring at a white four-wheel drive, head on, ten meters away—then none.

The car jolted, spinning now, deeper into the wrong side of the highway.

The second hit came from the side. The prius crumpled. Elodie didn't even have time to scream.

* * *

"A dog?" Elodie could hear her husband saying in a sharp tone that was very unlike him. Markus was usually courteous to a fault. "You're telling me this was caused by a *dog?*"

A woman's voice interrupted him. "Mr. Black. As I was saying. Based on the CCTV footage, a dog attempted to cross the intersection, yes. But what *caused* the accident was the car that swerved to avoid it. An automated vehicle."

"That doesn't make sense," Markus snapped. "I work with this kind of technology. An autocar wouldn't swerve to avoid an animal. That's a core feature of their programming. Human life over animal life. Every time."

An air-conditioned breeze tickled Elodie's nose. She wanted to sneeze but couldn't.

Where am I?

Not at home. She knew that much. She lay on a hard mattress, swaddled in a scratchy cotton blanket. Behind her closed eyes, she could see the glare of harsh overhead lighting. A steady beep sounded somewhere to her left.

Then the memories came back. Rushing to church. The phone in her hand. The sudden swerve, her overcorrection, and her heel slipping off the brake...

"Well, Mr. Black, all I can tell you is that this one apparently did," the woman said. "Police are investigating. The car manufacturer, too. It's been on the news."

"We'll sue," Markus growled.

She sighed. "I imagine you'd have a case. But your wife is going to be fine, Mr. Black. Just bruises and a mild concussion. She'll be a little groggy from the pain medication, that's all."

"Markus," Elodie whispered. It came out as barely more than a whisper, but she immediately felt the energy in the room shift as Markus rushed over and grabbed her hand. His calloused palm closed over hers and squeezed gently.

I'm okay. Everything's okay.

Clearing her throat, she tried again, squinting up at him through her lashes. Everything around them was washed out and clinical, but her husband looked wonderfully warm— she drank in the sight of his russet curls and freckled arms, tanned from working on the landscaping of their new house. He grinned at her, lawsuit seemingly forgotten.

Elodie smiled back. "Can we go home?"

He laughed—a shaky sound that told her how scared he'd been. "Thought you'd never ask."

* * *

As Markus drove through the X15 tunnel, Elodie studied his profile carefully, taking in his unruly hair, strong chin and cheekbones, and eyes slightly hollowed out from lack of sleep. Something was bothering him. She could tell by the lines around his mouth and the tight grip he kept on the wheel of his Tesla SUV.

"What is it, babe?" she asked softly.

Markus glanced sideways at her before returning his gaze to the tunnel. "Nothing."

Elodie chuckled. "Usually it's you who says *what's wrong* and me who says *nothing,* even though it's always something. Talk to me."

Markus sighed. "Today was rough. When the call came, they didn't tell me what had happened to you or that you were okay. Just that you were in an accident and being taken to Saint Peter's."

He paused then, and glanced longingly at the screen that dominated the Tesla's dashboard—as though wishing for a distraction. Elodie prickled. What was her husband not saying?

"And?" she prompted.

Markus exhaled in a rush as they exited the tunnel and slipped onto the freeway. Elodie rummaged for her sunglasses; the late afternoon light was dazzling.

"And," he said slowly, "I'd been angry at you. After this morning. I was feeling sorry for myself because it sometimes feels like you always put everything else first. Church, friends, your mother. I was thinking that I wanted—"

The car ahead of them braked sharply, and Markus followed suit, jostling Elodie a little.

"Sorry," he said, reaching for her hand. "Sorry. Shit. I'll be more careful."

Elodie patted his hand. "I'm fine, honestly. Today might have been started by that other car, but it was also my own fault. I was looking at my phone."

Markus recoiled. "What? You promised you didn't do that anymore."

Turning off the eastbound exit, their car glided silently onto a tree-lined street full of townhouses. *Nearly home.*

"I don't, usually," Elodie snapped. "Just at the lights."

"At the—"

Markus stopped himself, making the last turn onto their street and into the brand-new driveway of their townhouse. The little front garden looked charming, complete with a neatly-trimmed viburnum hedge and bird bath. When Markus finished painting the front steps, the facade would be perfect.

As they waited for the garage door to open, Markus turned to her in earnest. He looked properly angry now, though he was trying not to be. "At the lights? Like *where you had your accident?*"

"Don't lecture, and don't deflect," Elodie said. "I've already learned my lesson. Tell me what you were going to say before— about what you wanted."

Tell me something real, for once, she thought. *Not lecturing, not pontificating about some new technology or abstract scientific theory or philosophical principle. Tell me how you feel.*

After every argument, every tense silence—Elodie wondered. Were they happy?

Markus slumped in his seat. The garage door was open now, but he made no move to pull into their cluttered garage, which was still full of all the detritus of their previous life at the rental house. Neither one of them had found time to sort through it.

"I wanted," he said slowly, "for you to stay, for once. I wanted you to *want* to stay. Like I was saying before you left, I understand that church is important to you. But to me—it doesn't make sense. With so little evidence, how can you be so sure that your beliefs are right? Amongst all the others who believe different and mutually exclusive things?"

He was warming to his subject now, slipping back into the well-worn groove of devil's advocate. Elodie suppressed the urge to roll her eyes.

Markus continued. "If the endgame of religion is to find oneself in Heaven, then surely the best insurance policy is to just go Catholic. If it turns out Jesus was just some con man and another prophet was right, then I may suffer a little, but I'll be covered."

Elodie groaned aloud. "Religion isn't an insurance policy!"

"Are you sure about that, babe?" Markus raised his eyebrows. "Why else would people adhere to rules created by someone they've never met other than to reach an endgame? In this case, Heaven?"

Grabbing her bag, Elodie jumped out of the car and stalked inside, letting the door slam behind her. She heard the near-silent whirr as Markus parked the Tesla, then the groaning of the outdated garage door as it closed. She made a mental note to have it serviced.

Her husband followed her up the hall and into the kitchen. With their renovation recently completed, it looked lovely, if a little bare—all brushed gunmetal chrome and white marble, with four elegant gold stools lined up at the breakfast bar.

Behind her, Markus was still talking. "For instance, say I choose Catholicism, but it turns out that the Quran is the one true word? Then I'll go to hell, but that would only be temporary since Allah promises to bring people out from the fire and admit them into Paradise. Not quite as bad as the eternal flames of the Catholic God, don't you think, darling? Doesn't it make sense to go with the religion that wields the bigger stick?"

Elodie leaned on the counter as she pulled off her heels. She almost didn't answer, but Markus fell silent, raising his eyebrows as though challenging her to engage.

"You already know my thoughts on the matter," she said.

"As a matter of fact, I don't know. I don't believe you've actually said—you just don't like talking about it," Markus said, leaning against the door frame, his arms crossed over his chest.

Elodie straightened and smoothed out her dress. "Because this isn't *talking*, Markus. This is just you being a shit and trying to get a rise out of me while deflecting from having to answer the original question."

Markus frowned. "So, you pretty much just want me to shut up and come to church, huh?"

Elodie put her hands on her hips and glared. "We've had this conversation before. It usually goes along these lines..."

She cleared her throat before putting on her best impersonation of him. "Of course, it may be possible for me to be a Buddhist and a Catholic, since they aren't mutually exclusive. It may also be possible to reach the Jewish Heaven as a Catholic, since the Jewish Talmud says the righteous of all nations may enter. Gosh, I really don't know why the Christians had to make their happy place so exclusive, do you?"

Markus looked crestfallen, which only led Elodie to believe she'd hit the nail on the head.

"I might also have mentioned that the Hindu faith would only put me in hell until I'm reincarnated," he said, a little sheepishly.

"Yeah, well," Elodie snapped, "I think we've both made our points, and now I'm going to bed."

She grabbed her shoes and bag, fully intending to storm upstairs and lock him out of the bedroom. Then she paused and planted a conciliatory kiss on his cheek. He pulled her in for a quick hug.

"Join the Catholics if you must," she said in a gentler voice. "Just try and get the front steps painted tomorrow. Archer and Kayla are coming over next weekend, remember?"

* * *

Markus watched with appreciation as his wife's beautiful form disappeared up the stairs. She'd called his bluff; Elodie knew perfectly well he wasn't joining any religion.

Markus turned on the news. The perfectly coiffed newsreader seemed especially chirpy this evening: "Forget GDP! New Zealand is prioritizing *gross national happiness*."

His mind drifted, arriving back on Elodie and her Sunday dress. It was truly an irreproachable garment, modest, covering down to the knee, but it had hugged her sensational figure in a way that struck him as sexier than something more revealing. Idly, he wondered if the guys at church noticed and immediately chided himself: of course they did.

Archer in particular.

Try as he might, Markus just couldn't shake the feeling that Archer—unfailingly polite, staunchly Christian, perpetually grinning Archer—was just a bit too into his wife. The man had a perfectly nice girlfriend, of course. And there was never any hard evidence, never anything to question without sounding insane. And yet, every time Markus saw him, he wanted to punch the guy in the mouth.

What made it worse was how friendly Elodie was. Not just to Archer but to everyone. The woman sought out social connections like it was a full-time job. What she didn't seem to realise was that her friendliness, combined with her looks, was bound to be misinterpreted. Sooner or later, someone was going to get the wrong idea.

If he were honest, he hadn't been complaining this morning just because he wanted to spend the day together—though of course he had. He'd been annoyed because he was *jealous*. Markus leaned back against the counter and rubbed his eyes. Who was this anxious person, the guy who talked too much just to get a rise out of his wife, texted her when she wasn't five minutes out the door, and lectured her as though she were a child? The guy who wanted to punch acquaintances for no apparent reason?

He had almost lost her today. Not just to church or her mother's demands—he had almost lost her permanently. Completely. Forever.

The thought made him nauseous. He took a deep breath, battling the urge to throw up in their brand new sink.

Life had become so protected these days, in large part because of the field he worked in. Advanced surveillance technology meant very low crime in urban areas. AI driver assistance in newer cars meant traffic accidents were increasingly rare. His digital life was seamlessly backed up in the cloud. It almost created the illusion that nothing could ever go wrong. Today had proven the opposite; he could lose Elodie at any time. More than that—he *would* one day lose her. This terror, this nausea that he was feeling right now? One day it would be real.

Something stirred in the back of his mind. An idea. Ridiculous, on the face of it. But then—

Grabbing the phone from his pocket, Markus typed out a message. *Meet me at the lab early tomorrow. I just decided on our next project.*

CHAPTER TWO

COME ALL YE FAITHFUL

PRESENT DAY

"Remind me why we're going to all this trouble?" Markus grumbled as he uncorked the wine, pouring overpriced merlot into the tall, glass contraption Elodie had conjured up from the back of a cupboard. A *decanter*. Supposedly essential for good red, something to do with aeration, though he'd be damned if he could taste the difference.

"Because since moving, we hardly ever hang out with anyone," Elodie replied as she artfully arranged cheese and figs on a platter.

"So?"

"I want to make more friends," she said simply. "It's important to me."

Markus was baffled. "You have tons of friends."

"No, I don't. Not really. I know a lot of people, but that's not the same thing."

Casting a look in his wife's direction, Markus thought she was positively glowing. While he always knew she was beautiful, her excitement amplified it. He found himself unable to focus on the preparations for the visitors; he was distracted by everything Elodie. Her blonde hair cascaded in waves over her shoulders. She was bathed in a golden halo of sunlight which streamed in from the kitchen window. Then there was the knockout red dress that accentuated every curve of her slim figure. Markus felt a rush of pride in his wife. She had run around like a madwoman all day, cleaning and cooking, arranging flowers and making sure everything looked just so. As much as he grumbled and complained, he had to admit the house looked great, and Markus reminded himself of how hard they worked to establish themselves in what she called *an aspirational lifestyle*. Why shouldn't Elodie show it off? If it makes her happy, he could make it through one boring evening with her friends.

Wanting to make up for his sullen mood, Markus scooped up the last of the cheese wrappers and gave the counter a quick wipe, leaving it elegantly bare except for the platter and a few clean wine glasses.

"Thank you," Elodie said, her eyebrow raised. Markus smiled and wrapped his arms around her, squeezing gently. For a brief moment he thought she'd pull away, but Elodie relaxed in his arms and looked up at him with a soft smile.

There you are.

"Everyone likes you, babe," he said, choosing his words carefully. "All that shit with your mother, it makes you think people are so critical of you, but you don't see what everyone else sees. A stunning,"—he kissed her on the cheek—"smart and amazing woman."

Elodie rolled her eyes and pulled away, the compliment washing off her like water on polished stone, though he could see that she was smiling. "Even if that's true, it's not Mum's fault."

Markus turned away so she couldn't see his reaction. It mystified him why his wife constantly made excuses for the shitty way her mother treated her. By all accounts, Methel had had a rough life. Her father had been a drunk with a fierce temper. She'd married young, with the dream of having a big family and doing things better than her own parents had, but that wasn't to be; Methel and Antonio would only have two children, and one died just three weeks after he was born. So Elodie was an only child, the center of her mother's warped universe. Elodie thought their relationship was normal, but Markus disagreed. Methel's drinking, her depression, her rages, her incessant demands, the savage critiques of her daughter disguised as love and concern... none of it was normal.

Markus believed in determinism, so intellectually he knew that Methel's abusive behaviour towards Elodie wasn't really a choice. Everything a person did was dictated by previously existing causes, like their own trauma, what ideas they'd been exposed to, and even their DNA. Emotionally, though, he did blame his mother-in-law somewhat. Pre-determined or not, the woman had passed the cycle of abuse on to her daughter, and Elodie struggled to deal with the fallout every day.

Just thinking about Methel riled him up. Markus momentarily considered a finger or two of bourbon before their guests' arrival. He found himself suddenly tense, as if tonight was some sort of test he hadn't studied for.

I'm being ridiculous. They're just church friends of Elodie's. It's not like I've never met them. I could do without Archer, but Kayla's always easy to talk to.

The doorbell rang, and his wife lit up like a firecracker. "They're here! Could you answer the door? I have to set out the breadsticks."

* * *

They gathered around the cheese board in the kitchen, Kayla cooing over the marble countertop and various high-end fixtures while Markus poured the wine. Elodie gazed around anxiously, scanning for some detail she'd forgotten, but everything looked perfect. She sipped her wine and tried to relax.

"So, it's real marble? You didn't want to go with quartz?" Kayla was asking. She looked typically glamorous in yellow Carolina Hererra. *A bit low cut*, Elodie thought. Kayla's long, brown hair was styled in waves that looked effortless, but they had probably taken at least an hour in a professional salon. Her lush eyelashes were fake, costing at least ninety dollars, and the sky-high heels were frankly ludicrous. She looked beautiful, but Elodie privately thought it was a bit much.

Markus shrugged. "Came with the house. We didn't see any point changing it." He sounded a little bored. Apparently, Kayla couldn't tell—she carried right on enthusing—but Elodie could. She said a quick mental prayer that her husband would behave himself tonight and not say anything controversial. As if reading her thoughts, he caught her eye and gave a reassuring wink.

Elodie carefully placed her glass on the counter, fearing if she gripped it any tighter it would shatter. She turned to Archer with a smile. He stood back, with his arms folded, and she realised with a thrill that he'd been looking at *her* while Kayla and Markus were talking. The knowledge made her uneasy, but there was also something else: a small seed of validation. His girlfriend was dressed to kill, but Archer wasn't looking at Kayla.

Feeling heat rise in her cheeks, she directed his attention to the platter. "You should try the Gouda, Archer."

"Don't mind if I do," he replied, leaning forward and picking up the delicate cheese knife. As he did, Elodie allowed herself a moment to look at him closely. There was no denying he was handsome. Like his girlfriend, Archer always dressed well. He had the casual elegance of a guy who came from money. His clothes were tailored, and his shoes had to be Italian-made soft leather. He wore his hair slicked back in that classic way made possible only by an expensive haircut which must require frequent upkeep. In Elodie's opinion, Archer was the sort of man who would have made her mother happy: handsome, courteous, Christian. A son-in-law Methel could have bragged about to her church friends.

On the other hand, while Markus was an excellent provider, he was used to having to work hard for his money. He often dressed as if they were still scrimping and saving. That and his tendency to say whatever was on his mind often rubbed Methel the wrong way. Elodie could never decide if this dynamic bothered her or if it was what attracted her to Markus in the first place. Perhaps it was a little of both.

Reminding herself to stop comparing the two men, Elodie took another swallow of wine as Kayla's chatter turned into gushing praise of their silver glass splashback.

"How's work?" Archer asked, clearly not interested in discussing the kitchen decor. "What's this about you saving the world?"

Elodie felt a warmth spread up her neck and into her cheeks. "I'm hardly saving the world. I'm only a junior research associate."

Archer sipped his wine thoughtfully. "Don't sell yourself short. I hear you enjoy it?"

A smile tugged at the corners of her mouth. "I do. It's fascinating work, at least in my opinion."

"I'm sure it is. What is it exactly that you're working on?" Archer asked.

Elodie flashed him a quick glance from beneath her eyelashes, trying to gauge if he was genuinely interested or simply being polite. His gaze was steady, his smile encouraging.

"Well, our initial goal is to garner greater control over the weather, starting with electronic cloud seeding to manipulate rain patterns. If—no, *when* we achieve this, I believe we can take it further. Have a real impact on reducing climate change. The technology is funded by agriculture mostly, so we're starting there. But we're in talks with—" she stopped short, reminding herself that the information was still confidential. "Anyway, our systems are presently in a trial overseas."

"That's exciting!" Archer said. He seemed to mean it.

Elodie nodded. "It's hard to keep up with technology as it's progressing so fast, in ways that were unimaginable even five years ago. Eventually we'll be able to schedule rain the way we schedule trains. No more droughts, no more floods—we will eliminate natural disasters altogether while increasing the global agricultural yield. And that's only the beginning."

Elodie paused as she realised that Kayla and Markus had stopped talking and were also listening to her. Instantly, her insecurities took hold. "Try the Camembert, Kayla," she said awkwardly. "It's really good."

Her friend smiled broadly as she obliged. "I think it's brilliant what you're doing, Elodie. You're too modest. Tell Archer what you told me about the temperature."

Elodie hid behind her glass as she drank the last of her wine, buying herself a brief moment to think.

I love my job, but I must remember that, for many people, it's controversial. I didn't invite them over to discuss work.

Yet the others didn't seem as eager to let it drop.

"What about the temperature?" Archer asked, "You surely aren't suggesting your company will control that, too?"

"You'd better believe it." Markus jumped in before she could answer, his smile lighting up his features as he poured more wine into Elodie's glass. "Sooner than you think, too. They'll be able to control the Earth's temperature as easily as we turn the air conditioning up or down. Think of it. No more climate change unless it's beneficial. No more natural disasters. They'll create cyclones or stop them, depending on our needs."

Archer guffawed. There was no other word to describe his loud, incredulous laugh. "You must get asked this all the time, but for argument's sake, if we believe climate change is a natural phenomenon, then you'd be essentially creating man-made climate change and going against God's design."

"I don't pretend to know God's design," Elodie said earnestly, "but who's to say that this technology isn't God's design? To evolve a species to the point where they—we—can create a better existence for all? Every animal has an impact on their environment. This is not so different."

"I think it's wonderful," Kayla said. Elodie looked at her in surprise. It was rare that she contradicted Archer; perhaps the wine was going to her head. "If you ask me," Kayla continued, "whether climate change is man-made or natural, a lot of people are suffering from it. This will make everyone's lives better."

"And that's not *half* of what's coming in the next couple of decades," Markus said. "At Neural, we…"

"Let's go outside," Elodie interjected. "The sun's setting, and it's lovely out there this time of day. Markus, could we have another bottle?" She gave him a stern look, hoping it conveyed her message.

Please do not discuss your work with our guests.

Deciding it was high time for the light dinner party conversation she'd intended, Elodie commandeered the cheeseboard and made for the sliding patio door, which Archer opened for her with a courteous flourish. He pulled a wicker chair out for her, too, as though he were the host and their patio furniture belonged to him.

Kayla settled into her own chair without Archer's help and reached for a piece of fig before inspecting the little courtyard. "This is really lovely, Elodie. I'm happy for you. Your own home at last."

Elodie glanced at her friend, wondering if Archer had picked up on the slightly bitter tone in her voice. For months Kayla had tirelessly campaigned for Archer to move in with her—preferably *marry* her, and then move in with her, but moving in was better than nothing—and so far, Archer had remained impervious to her increasingly pointed suggestions.

As Markus returned with a freshly decanted bottle and began topping up everyone's drinks, Elodie felt a surge of warmth towards him. His devotion to her was something she took for granted. Markus couldn't get her to the altar quick enough, unlike Kayla and her failing attempts to force Archer into holy matrimony. Markus didn't have to tell her how much he loved her; it was evident in the way he entertained her friends—people he didn't particularly like. Elodie knew her husband would much rather be doing something else, but not once had he shown his reluctance. She made a mental note to find a way to make it up to him later.

Once Markus sat down with his own glass, Archer leaned forward, seemingly oblivious to the fact that Kayla was in the middle of talking to him. "So, Markus. You were saying?"

"Oh, yeah," Markus said, his expression brightening. "Depending on your familiarity with the science, this might sound incredible, so bear with me. At Neural, we're working on human immortality."

* * *

"You can't be serious."

Archer's tone was confident, bordering on derisive. Markus's mouth twitched into a smile—he couldn't help it. The surer of himself Archer was, the more fun this conversation would be.

"Very," he assured him. "You might have heard about some of our old projects, like the BMIR device?"

Kayla reached for another piece of cheese. "You know the one, honey. I told you about it. They controlled the movements of a rat just by *thinking*."

"That's the one," Markus said, "with the thoughts of a human operator. It was several years ago now."

Elodie sat rigid in her chair, looking a bit pale. Markus hoped the food wasn't disagreeing with her.

"Okay, so you controlled a rat. Very interesting. Doesn't seem related to immortality," Archer said.

"Admittedly, no," Markus agreed. "On the surface, none of it does. Most of the people working on this technology aren't thinking about the endgame. We have several projects on the go at any given time, mostly for high-end medical applications. Concurrently, we learn more about the capabilities of the human brain while increasing our scanning and computational power. Sometimes, we make small breakthroughs like the BMIR. But if we continue on this trajectory, immortality is where it's headed."

"Sure," Archer scoffed, "like scientists haven't claimed that before. Ever heard of the philosopher's stone?"

Markus chuckled. "I assure you, Archer, we'll see this within our lifetimes."

"Really?" Kayla asked, popping the piece of cheese in her mouth as she leaned against Archer.

"Absolutely. At the rate we're going, I'm confident we'll develop a detailed-enough scan of the human brain that we'll be able to map out the entirety of a person's neural connectome—everything that makes them who they are—and store it on a server." Markus paused, taking a sip of his wine.

"What, you mean like backing data up to the cloud?" Kayla asked.

"Essentially, yes, though in the initial stages it's more likely to be a data bank rather than the cloud. By storing the data held in our brains, we'll be immortal... theoretically at least. "

"And this is something you could do more than once?" Kayla asked incredulously. "You know, like a smartphone? You drop it in the toilet, it fries, you buy a new phone and restore the backup?"

Markus laughed. "You could think of it that way. Effectively, any memories between the last backup and the point of your death would be lost—as though you'd been under anaesthesia. But the restored version would be you in every other sense. Eventually, I'm sure people will back up automatically to the cloud, so that even that risk is eliminated."

"Hang on," Archer cut in. "This is all theoretical, right? You said no one at your company is *actively* working on this *backup* idea. So tell me, then: how do you expect to ultimately achieve this neural data bank?"

Elodie held her breath as she watched Markus lean forward and look Archer square in the eye. "The technology already exists. It becomes exponentially more powerful every year. "

Kayla cackled, pouring herself a third glass of wine. "If you ask me, it sounds like something from a sci-fi movie. I mean no offence, Markus, but it sounds *crazy.*"

"Crazy is an understatement," Archer said. "The Bible says that people can't engineer or transfer that which is spirit. So you may be able to copy data from someone's mind, but you will never create an immortal copy of them."

Thwack.

Someone's shoe collided painfully with Markus's shin. He looked around, bewildered, and caught Elodie's glare. It dawned on him a little too late: she was worried his work might seem *blasphemous.* Why didn't that possibility occur to him earlier?

To be fair, it hadn't been an issue before, when he came home and told her about their success in mapping a roundworm brain—or when that brain scan was successfully transferred to a robot, which moved around like a real roundworm. That had been a great day; he and Elodie had gone out to celebrate after work. She was pleased when Neural greenlit the funding to develop that technology further, with the end goal of mapping human brains. So why would it bother her if the resulting data was used for its obvious purpose? Was it so different to extending life in other ways, like putting a pacemaker in the heart or manipulating gene sequences to treat disease?

If the research and its applications had bothered her, she had never said so. He wondered what else she was not saying. Markus stared at his wife, so beautiful in her red dress, still sipping her first glass of merlot with careful restraint. Something painful stirred in his chest: a feeling like the dream he used to have as a kid of showing up to school in his pyjamas. Or maybe it was more like the memory of being drunk at a party, talking and talking, spilling your guts, only to realise too late that the other person was sober and not revealing anything in return. For years now, he'd been talking to Elodie in this way:

detailing his innermost thoughts and preoccupations, all of which amounted to *who he was*. But she had remained a sealed-off universe of different personas. The wife who listened to the details of his workday, made a few comments and changed the subject—that was who she was in relation to him. But she had other sides to her, like the slavishly dutiful daughter who'd spend the entirety of her weekend running errands for her mother, or the ardent Christian he caught glimpses of on Sunday as she dressed up and ran out the door. It was entirely possible there were still more sides to Elodie, and perhaps he didn't know them well at all.

Markus put his glass down and was silent for a long moment. He should probably just end the conversation there, go back to talking about the kitchen fixtures. But what—to be frank—was the point? Why spend your life engaged in dull, safe conversations no one actually cared about? Not even Kayla could be *that* interested in splashbacks.

What the hell, he thought. "Archer, you're a man of God?" he said cautiously.

Archer shrugged, as if to say *of course*.

"So, you'd be familiar with the part of Genesis where it talks about the tree of life and the tree of knowledge."

"Sure," Archer drawled, "God forbade Adam and Eve to eat from the tree of knowledge. But they did, and so mankind fell into imperfection and sin."

"That's the one," Markus agreed. "But why? I mean, why make the tree, only to forbid them to eat from it? I always found that strange."

Kayla chimed in. "The tree was there so that mankind had a choice to obey God. But it was forbidden because it meant we would become like God, knowing good and evil."

Markus grinned at her gratefully. "So, I realise that everyone interprets these things differently. But to me, those trees sound like a metaphor for the evolution of life. Per the Bible itself, by eating from the tree, we become like gods. My personal theory is that when humans evolved from primates, to have knowledge of right and wrong, that was when we ate from the tree of knowledge; when we achieve immortality, that's when we'll eat from the tree of life and become truly godlike. The last gods. The apex of evolution."

"There's a couple of problems with your theory," Archer said firmly. "Firstly, humans evolved from Adam and Eve, not from primates. Secondly, there will only ever be one God. So, we might be *like* him in knowing good and evil, but we'll never achieve immortality. Humans aren't meant to live forever—in their earthly form, anyway."

"Yeah, but we're not exactly talking about an earthly form," Markus said, making an effort to keep his tone light, though Archer's endless smugness was rubbing him the wrong way. "Theoretically, it's just data. And don't quote me on this, but I think it says somewhere in Genesis that *nothing they propose to do will be withheld from them.* That sounds to me like, if we seek immortality, we might just find it. When tempted by the tree of life, we will eat from it. Most religions agree that life on Earth is merely a preparation for life in Heaven. Maybe as we become God-like—when we remove all that is considered evil from ourselves and from the universe, perhaps we will be pure enough to be accepted into Heaven."

"That's *such* an interesting theory," Kayla said. "Of course, it's pretty different from the interpretation we follow, but I'll take the fulfillment of Bible prophecy however it comes. Stranger things have happened!"

Archer said nothing as he stared at Markus, who picked up his glass of wine and took a triumphant sip.

* * *

As Markus fired up the barbecue, Elodie excused herself and took the opportunity to escape to the bathroom. Peering at herself in the mirror, she was alarmed to find herself looking peaked. She turned the faucet on and splashed cold water on her face before bracing her hands against the basin and forcing herself to take a deep breath.

You're just being silly. Why worry about a little conversation *over wine? If Kayla and Archer are real friends, they'll accept Markus's unorthodox ideas. I would do it for them.*

Yet, Elodie knew that wasn't the only reason she felt so faint. She hadn't realised that having Kayla and Markus together in close quarters would leave her feeling like she was teetering on a knife's edge. Kayla had sworn to keep her secret, and under normal circumstances, Elodie knew she could trust her. But the more Kayla drank, the more she tried to glitter before Archer, the more she seemed slightly out of character.

"Stranger things have happened?" Why would Kayla say that when it was obvious Markus's theory was incompatible with their faith?

The randomness of Kayla's statement made her worry what else her friend might blurt out. With trembling hands, Elodie quickly patted her face with the towel, touched up her lipstick and headed back out into the hall, where Archer appeared out of the shadows.

Elodie barely suppressed a cry. *"Archer!* You scared me!"

He held his hands out in a gesture of innocence. "Sorry, sorry. Just coming to see if you're okay. You weren't saying much out there."

"I'm fine," she said brightly. "Just a little tired, maybe. It's been a long week."

He ducked his head until she met his gaze. There was something strange in his expression—she tried to tell herself it was concern, but instinct told her it was something else. Archer didn't seem like the sort of man who considered other people's wellbeing. More than once, Elodie had witnessed his poor treatment of Kayla: affable but oblivious, disinterested until the matter at hand concerned *him.* It was why her friend was sitting outside, chugging down what would be her fourth glass of wine while putting on a big show of laid-back happiness that no one was buying. Elodie could understand why—without explicitly saying it, Archer definitely gave the impression he'd quickly disappear if things with Kayla stopped being fun.

Yet here he was, looking at her with an expression she'd never seen on his face before...

Very odd.

He crossed his arms and leaned against the wall. "It must be difficult."

"What's that?" Elodie asked as she began to step past him.

"Being married to someone who doesn't share your faith."

She stopped in her tracks and turned her head, looking at him with trepidation. "Markus has his ideas, and I have mine. Part of loving someone is respecting their decisions and opinions, wouldn't you say?"

Her voice sounded weak, nervous. She went to move past him, but Archer didn't budge. Wasn't this a bit... inappropriate? Shouldn't they both be outside, saying things that could be said in front of their partners?

He touched her arm, and Elodie felt afraid. Not because his grip was rough—the opposite, in fact. Because it was gentle.

"I want you to know," he said, "I'm here for you if you ever need to talk. I know what it's like, being with someone who has a different worldview. It can be lonely. Isolating."

Elodie slowly turned her head and looked at him, needing to determine how serious he was. Within seconds she realised he wasn't teasing. Not just making polite conversation. He meant what he said—and he also meant the things he wasn't saying. For a moment, she could hardly breathe; her throat was dry. She swallowed, and stared back at him.

It is lonely. The thought came unbidden, and it hurt more than Elodie could have anticipated.

He stood so close that she could feel his warm breath on her face. For a long moment their eyes stayed locked, and she had a sudden urge to confide in him, to admit how hard marriage could be, and how alone she felt most of the time. She wanted to tell Archer how she'd never felt good enough for anyone except God—and recently she had lost even that. But this was not the time, the place, and definitely not the person to discuss her feelings with. She pulled her arm away.

Not a moment too soon. The sliding door opened, and Markus appeared at the far end of the hallway. He went very still, and Elodie suddenly saw herself through his eyes. She plastered on a broad smile.

"Bathroom is the second door to the left," she said brightly. Archer nodded and disappeared around the corner. She looked back at Markus, but he was gone.

Elodie swallowed hard. *What was that? What would have happened if Markus hadn't walked in? Would Archer have tried to kiss me?*

The thought filled her with horror. It would destroy everything she was trying so hard to create: a nice, respectable life with Markus and good friendships within the church.

Though, if she were honest with herself, there was more to it. That passing moment had felt uncomfortably similar to the night she most wanted to forget. Tonight, more than ever, the memory haunted her; she closed her eyes, and in an instant, Elodie could have sworn she was back in Hawaii.

In moments like this one, she wished that it was possible to upload minds. Not for immortality, like Markus wanted, but so that memories could be deleted.

One in particular.

The memory felt like it rightly belonged to someone else—some other woman in some other life. Before Hawaii, Elodie would have sworn up and down that she'd never be unfaithful to her husband. Seven years with Markus and she'd never once been tempted. What she craved more than anything was simple friendship, which always seemed more difficult to come by than romance. It was why she'd accepted Kayla's invitation to tag along with her friends on a girls' trip to Hawaii in the first place. The holiday had been awkward from the start because the other women knew each other far better than Elodie knew

Kayla. She was the odd one out; insecure and out of sorts, until the last night of their trip when a kind of madness came over her. She'd enjoyed the attention of a local man, thinking it was harmless, until everything went too far. The shame of committing a mortal sin was something she would carry to her grave.

Beyond the sin, what bothered Elodie the most was how she had traded fleeting pleasure for long-term suffering. She couldn't believe she had been so foolish. At first she'd blamed Kayla, wondering why her friend had not stepped in to save her once the night started getting out of hand. But Kayla was her friend, and Elodie was a grown woman. She could hardly blame Kayla for her mistakes.

How could you ever have been so foolish?

Naturally, her thoughts turned to God. He knew everything about her—from the anxiety and rejection of her childhood to the endless need for approval she felt as an adult. He knew her sincere longing for genuine friendship and connection, and how much it hurt when that closeness eluded her. In fact, God knew her every thought and could predict her every action. So, in the aftermath of Hawaii, she felt almost betrayed.

Why did He not guide me toward a better choice?

Deep down, though, she knew the answer. Just as God put the tree of knowledge in the garden of Eden, giving Adam and Eve the choice to obey him or not, so it was in ordinary life. God gave free will to his children. He might know what they would choose to do, but He did not dictate their actions and, thereby, make humankind into obedient automatons. Good or bad, their choices were theirs to make. So, this mistake was hers, and hers alone.

Hearing Archer flush the toilet, Elodie pulled herself together and hurried back to the kitchen. Her brief interlude had provided her with the clarity to determine exactly what she needed to do. Good intentions were not enough, not anymore. Knowledge was the key. Knowledge was power, as the truism went. Elodie realised that if she had understood herself better, Hawaii would never have happened. She would have known her craving for approval made her vulnerable, how fleeting the pleasure of validation would be—and how deep and insidious the guilt. God may not intervene in her mistakes, but self-knowledge could. Knowledge would make her a better and happier person. Perhaps the same could be said for the world; if humankind could know what God knew, they wouldn't make mistakes.

Retrieving her glass from the counter, Elodie busied herself in the kitchen until Archer went back outside. She watched through the glass sliding door as he joined Markus on the patio. Unintentionally, they mirrored each other, facing off across the table with their arms crossed. *The man of God and the man of knowledge.* It was a fanciful thought, of course—Archer was hardly a paragon of virtue, and Markus's field of expertise was limited. Yet she couldn't help but wonder whose version of the future would come to pass.

At the current rate of progress, if she was lucky, she might just find out.

CHAPTER THREE

THE WAGES OF SIN IS DEATH

ONE YEAR LATER

*T**hump.*

Something landed on the front porch, hard enough to rattle the windows. Poised over the frying pan, attempting to retrieve a tiny piece of shell from his rapidly scrambling eggs, Markus paused and raised his eyebrows at Elodie.

"What was *that*?"

His wife shrugged and gave him a small smile over the rim of her coffee mug. "Ordered anything online lately?"

Markus gave up on the shell and continued stirring. "Yeah, but we always send things to the office, not here. Mind checking?"

Elodie sighed and set down her mug. Dark circles lined her beautiful blue eyes. She hadn't been sleeping well. Markus worried that it was his fault; they'd been in the spotlight lately, and he hadn't been around as much, as he'd wanted to shield her from it.

Inwardly, he cursed *The Daily Reporter*—the first outlet to pick up on what he'd thought was a fairly innocuous press release from Neural.

IMMORTALITY IN HIS HANDS, the headline had screamed, along with a photo of Markus from his mother's birthday party last year. He'd arrived late, straight from work, still wearing his lab coat. In the photo, he looked a mess—flushed, bleary-eyed, in need of a haircut. The classic mad scientist. That was the angle the papers had taken, and they were sticking with it despite his repeated attempts to clarify the innocuous nature of his research.

Nobody wanted to hear that all they were doing was increasingly accurate brain scanning, with the aim of regenerating a human brain in much the same way that other labs were already doing heart or lung tissue. Theoretically, the same technology could one day be used to copy and store a human brain in digital form—heavy emphasis on the *theoretically* part—but that kind of news didn't drive clicks. No, the papers wanted the story to be that he was on the cusp of playing God. They had blown it way out of proportion. And it was stressing out his wife.

Elodie sighed, retied the sash on her sky blue bathrobe, and shuffled down the hallway. She flung the front door open a little too hard, and Markus winced. Was she angry with him?

A long silence followed. Markus plated up the eggs.

When Elodie finally came back inside, holding a large cardboard box, her face was entirely drained of colour. Her wide eyes lifted from the box to Markus, and she said quietly, "Call the police."

Markus dropped the oily frypan into the sink. "What?"

"I said," Elodie hissed, *"call the fucking police."*

She placed the open box on their kitchen counter. Inside it was a human skull. A *real* one, Markus thought. Not plastic. He didn't quite know how he could tell.

Hands shaking, Elodie held out an A4 piece of paper. Two lines of text were centred on the page in a generic font. Markus squinted at them.

Everyone dies, the note read. *Some sooner than others. End it now.*

"What?" Markus said, his voice coming out strangely high-pitched. "What's that supposed to mean?"

Elodie glared at him, bracing herself against the counter. "It's clearly a threat against your life."

Markus dropped the note into the box and scrubbed his face with his hands. "We don't know that. It's a bit ambiguous."

Elodie laughed; a harsh, terrified bark of a sound. "Don't be obtuse. All that news coverage? The death threats online? This is an escalation. It's getting out of hand."

Markus started pacing the kitchen. "Okay. Assume you're right. How could a stranger know where we live? This address isn't publicly listed; I make sure of it. Only a few people actually know we're here. My parents, your mum, Jon and Brandon, Kayla and Archer—"

He stopped short, and Elodie's eyes narrowed. "Don't even think of blaming this on Archer. He would never."

Markus barely resisted the urge to roll his eyes. Actually, he was pretty sure Archer would *love* an opportunity to drive a wedge between them, particularly in relation to Markus's work.

"Are you sure, babe?" he asked. "Because, outside of family, Archer and Kayla are the only ones who have this address. Our families know not to share it. And I have a hard time imagining Kayla being involved in this. Didn't you say she moved to Canada after their breakup?"

"Toronto, yes," Elodie said flatly. Her eyes lingered on the box. "But frankly, I think you're being ridiculous. Someone could get our address any number of ways. You could have been followed from Neural. Archer warned us when you started down this road—"

Archer, Archer, Archer. Markus wanted to break something. "Oh, Archer, the professional ethicist?"

"Don't be snide," Elodie snapped. "And stop projecting. You want someone to blame for the fact we're now getting death threats at home? Look in the mirror. I'm going to Mum's."

With that, she flounced out of the kitchen. Her small frame and fluffy blue robe did nothing to make her less intimidating. Markus knew better than to follow.

Sighing, he turned and scraped his wife's eggs into the garbage disposal.

As Elodie pulled into Methel's flower-lined driveway, she noticed that her mother had made some changes around the house. A familiar red couch sat on the verge for council pickup, along with several large boxes of junk. Out front, the peppermint tree had been removed, leaving a gaping hole in the space to the right of the carport. The sight caused Elodie's throat to constrict. She'd spent countless hours under that tree, playing games, climbing, putting the thin leaves under her tongue to suck out the oily mint flavour. The tree had been planted in honour of Alex, her older brother who didn't survive in the womb.

Gathering her bags, Elodie climbed out of the car and made her way to the house. *Should have called ahead*, she realised. There was never any knowing what mood her mother might be in. There was irony in the fact that Elodie had lost her temper and come here, of all places; here, where countless times she had sat on the step under this very carport, anxiously waiting for Methel to come home from her own mother's house.

Oh well. It would be awkward to turn back now. Elodie hoisted the overnight bag over her shoulder and rang the doorbell.

"Coming," Methel shouted from somewhere at the back of the house. Elodie heard her shuffle down the hallway, swearing as she tried to locate her keys. The morning news was on in the background.

Finally, the heavy wooden door swung open.

Methel stood behind the security screen and stared. She was still in her nightgown. Her hair was a mess—not just mussed from sleep but neglected, with the usual sharp bob grown past her shoulders, and the immaculate honey blonde now showing grey at the roots.

"Mum," Elodie said, instantly feeling guilty. She'd left it too long between visits. "Are you okay?"

"I've been trying to reach you," her mother said sharply. "Having a clear-out. You didn't call me back, so it's all out there."

She gestured toward the items on the verge.

Elodie looked over her shoulder. Was that her old lava lamp sticking out of one of the boxes?

"Sorry," she said, shifting the weight of the bag on her shoulder. "There's been a lot going on. Can I come in?"

"Sure," Methel sniffed. There was a click as the screen door unlocked.

Feeling strangely chastened, Elodie stepped inside. The house smelled as it always did, of tea, cigarette smoke and lemon cleaning spray, but something in the atmosphere had shifted. Elodie walked through the cluttered kitchen and down the hallway toward her old room.

She stopped short in the doorway. It was... empty. Not just of her things but Alex's as well. The corner of the room that had once been a sort of shrine to her brother was now completely clear, with just a dressing table and empty clothes rack in the corner. Elodie's old bed was still there, but with a new coverlet, and without her old pillows and stuffed toys. It looked like a guest room.

Elodie dumped her bags and returned to the kitchen, where Methel was busily making tea. Her mother looked marginally more like herself—she'd changed into a printed day dress and brushed her hair, but still, the off-kilter feeling remained. She was avoiding meeting Elodie's gaze.

"Mum," Elodie said cautiously, "what's going on? What happened to everything?"

She felt a familiar sense of unease stirring.

Methel sighed heavily, bashing a tea bag against the side of her favourite china cup. "Nothing. Just high time I started living for myself, that's all. Nearly thirty years, utterly devoted to being a parent—and my one living child is too busy to call me back. I'm thinking of taking on a boarder from the university. Would be nice," here she paused for dramatic effect, "to have some company around here."

"Mum," Elodie repeated. It was almost dizzying, how Methel could make everything about herself. "There's been a lot going on. If you'd seen the news—"

Methel dropped the teaspoon with a clatter. Her face, a lined version of Elodie's, was tight with anguish. "I saw."

And? Elodie thought. *Can this be about me, for once? About what I'm feeling?*

"That husband of yours," her mother hissed. "His work. It's apostasy. An insult to God."

Elodie's eyes drifted to the heavy wooden cross above the kitchen sink. It had loomed, large and foreboding, over her childhood, always there to remind her of her sins, of all the ways she disappointed her mother. All the ways she fell short compared to what her brother would have done.

"Mum," Elodie said again. She felt herself deflating, shrinking. "He's trying to *help* people."

Funny that she should find herself defending Markus, when she'd come here to escape him.

"Helping them straight to Hell," Methel snapped.

Elodie heard her phone ringing from her bedroom—*the guest room*, she corrected herself. Probably Markus calling to apologise. He always did, even when Elodie knew, deep down, that she was overreacting.

Just like her father had, every time Methel flew into her rages and abandoned them for hours or days. He would always apologise, and make the tea exactly how she liked it, and make himself scarce until the storm blew over. He'd kowtowed to her mother until he died.

Elodie sighed. This wasn't what she wanted for herself and Markus. She really shouldn't have come.

The call went to voicemail. Markus frowned and slid the phone back into his pocket. No telling when his wife would forgive him, though she generally did—Elodie just returned without comment, acting as though the argument had never happened.

They needed to talk. They probably needed therapy.

He pulled into his parking space in the Neural basement, letting the Tesla handle the tight maneuver between his VP's car and the cement pillar.

An unfamiliar car sat opposite him in the near-empty lot. New staff, probably—the company was growing so fast that he couldn't keep track. He made a mental note to seek them out and say hello. It was important to maintain a personal relationship with his team.

Retrieving his coat, Markus slid out in the narrow space between his car and the pillar, already thinking ahead to this morning's meeting with a potential investor. If they could just secure more funding—

A hand slammed over his face. Pain exploded across his nose and mouth as it clamped down hard, pressing a towel into him, blocking his airways.

Markus struggled furiously, feeling a second pair of hands grab his arms. *The pillar,* he thought. *They were waiting behind the pillar.*

He barely registered the shock before his vision faded to black.

CHAPTER FOUR

BY THE GRACE OF GOD

Markus regained consciousness with his face pressed against cold tile. Every part of his body ached. He tried to move, but his arms wouldn't obey—after struggling for a moment, he realised they were tied behind his back. He tried to wriggle his fingers but couldn't feel them.

The room he was in was pitch black and smelled faintly of mold, like a bathroom without proper ventilation. A fan whirred somewhere overhead. The whine seemed to drill into his skull.

Markus groaned loudly, then stopped as he heard something move. Lights blinked on—bright white, dazzling. He was staring across a beige tile floor. When his eyes adjusted, he saw that he was in a dingy and sparsely furnished apartment. A blue couch sat near the middle of the room, and in front of it, an old-style television. The only window was small and high.

Basement, he thought, heart sinking. *Hard to escape.*

The sudden sound of a door opening caused terror to flood through him. He tried to leap up but could only manage a weak flail against the cold tile.

A pair of legs descended down the stairs leading to the small kitchenette area. Markus squinted. He wasn't sure what he was expecting of his kidnappers, but this certainly wasn't it. A woman came into view: small, thin, and barefoot in a pair of cut-off denim shorts and a ratty old t-shirt. She looked to be university age or slightly older. Her dark hair was long and pulled back into a messy ponytail. *She's pretty*, he thought.

A man followed close behind. He looked taller, older, meaner. He carried a cardboard box, which he set carefully down on the peeling linoleum benchtop. Then he looked at Markus and grinned.

"Didn't listen to our warning, huh?"

Markus felt his bowels turn to water. The skull had been a threat against his life; he knew that now. And he'd ignored it.

He cleared his throat. "You seriously expected me to find a skull on my doorstep and just... never go to work again?"

Despite his fear, the words came out angrily. He *was* angry. His temples throbbed. How dare these people do this to him?

Everybody dies, the note had said.

Were they going to kill him?

The girl bent over the sink, washed her face, and then filled a glass with water. She walked over to Markus and placed it on the tile floor. She crouched down to look him in the eye, her gaze piercing. Her eyes were a nice shade of hazel. "Can you sit up?"

Markus struggled into a sitting position. The blood slowly returning to his bound arms was hot agony.

She held the glass to his lips, carefully, and he drank. The pounding in his head eased a little.

"We *should* kill you," she said gently, as though she'd heard his thoughts. "Eric wanted to. I don't want to, but I know we should. Your research will be the end of humanity as we know it."

Her voice was soft, sincere. Her hand trembled as she withdrew the glass. She had some tattoos on her wrist, but he couldn't tell what they depicted.

Markus looked over at Eric. He had an unremarkable face—light brown hair, pale skin, standard features—but there was something hardened about him. Markus had no trouble believing that this guy wanted him dead.

"Can I get up?" Markus asked. "Sit on the couch or something?"

He needed to think, and being on the floor wasn't helping.

The young woman looked at Eric, who rolled his eyes and helped Markus up and over to the threadbare blue couch. It smelled vaguely of wet dog. He suspected they'd picked it up off the side of the road. Nothing about these people or this place suggested money. So, they probably weren't part of a large or well-coordinated group; they were likely rogue idealists, acting alone.

"Thank you," Markus said. He took a deep breath. "So, are you going to tell me why I'm here?"

He directed the question to the woman, who fiddled nervously with the hem of her t-shirt.

She again glanced at Eric, who sauntered back over, bringing his face uncomfortably close to Markus's. He smelled of cheap cigarettes—the kind that students went back to after the government banned vapes.

"My version," Eric drawled. "Sandy here wouldn't let me hit you with our van. Her version... well, like she said... end of humanity as we know it. You're fucking with the natural order, man. Playing God. It has to stop. And if you won't stop it, we'll stop it for you."

Markus considered this, trying to slow his breathing. A dozen potential answers raced through his head, but each one felt wrong. He decided to be honest. These people could easily kill him anyway. If he was going to die, he wanted it to be for the truth, not some badly patched together lie.

He took a deep breath. "Have you considered that the end of humanity as we know it is inevitable? And that it might not be such a bad thing?"

Eric snorted, but Sandy leaned in closer. Her eyes were trained on him like a rifle laser.

Markus took that as his cue to continue. "Yes, brain scanning technology has huge implications for our future. In theory, we could end up uploading human minds to the cloud. I know that's terrifying. It keeps me awake at night sometimes. But Neural is only the frontrunner in a race that's happening all over the world. If I don't succeed with this technology, it's only a matter of time before someone else does."

Eric laughed. "That's why we need to send a message."

"More to the point," Markus said quickly, "think of the upsides. Have you ever lost a loved one in death? This could put an end to that. In fact, the option to exist in data form could end *most* of the causes of human suffering. Death, pain, old age, poverty—when this technology reaches its full potential, all of that could be over if we choose to make it so. There's no limit to what we could do. Exponential increases in quality of life. Exponential increases in knowledge and wisdom. Far less strain on the world's physical resources. I'm not a religious man, but it could be—well, it could be like Heaven."

Sandy's eyes dropped. She'd moved her hands, and Markus could see her tattoo now; a delicate flower, and two dates separated by a hyphen.

When she looked up again, tears glimmered in her eyes. "That's such bullshit," she snapped. "You seriously want to sell us some utopian dream? My baby sister had leukemia, and there was a new drug that could have saved her. My family couldn't afford it, so she fucking *died*. So don't tell me your technology won't become one more thing that the rich can have and the poor can't. Except, this time, there won't be any revolution to rebalance the scales. They'll be untouchable. Immortal. They'll be like gods. *That's* what your technology will do. It'll create a plutocracy that lasts forever."

Markus stared back at her, wide-eyed, as it occurred to him that he was really going to die.

* * *

Elodie was almost home when she got a call from a strange number. She ignored it, as she usually did—calls from anyone outside her phone book were rarely welcome. Let them leave a message.

But the number called again. And again.

On the third try, she answered it, with no small amount of annoyance.

"Mrs. Black," a voice on the other end said without preamble. This is Detective Burnett with the Metropolitan Police Station. We need you to come in."

"Sorry?" Elodie asked, distracted, as she pulled into her driveway.

"We can send a car for you."

Elodie let her new Prius idle, shifting to hold the phone a little closer to her ear. "What is this about? The skull?"

"Really best that we discuss this at the station," the voice said. "We have a squad car two minutes from your location. They'll come pick you up."

"It's not really a good time—"

"Mrs. Black, they're on their way. Two minutes. Please don't move. We'll see you soon."

The line disconnected.

By the time she was dropped off at the station, Elodie was thoroughly disgruntled. She'd wanted them to take the threats seriously, of course—but she was meant to be headed to work. She had things to do. *Meetings.*

A barrel-chested man in uniform burst into reception and extended a meaty hand for her to shake. Elodie scowled, but politeness took over; she shook it.

"Detective Burnett?" she asked. "Please, can you tell me why I'm here?"

He paused, and then said, "My apologies, ma'am. Please follow me."

The detective scanned an ID card at a door to the right of the reception area, led her into a clinical interview room, and gestured for her to sit.

Elodie sat, glaring, as he disappeared down the hall and came back with a large tablet. He slid it across the table and sat opposite her as she swiped to view the screen.

As the grainy black and white image appeared, Elodie squinted. She was looking at a near-empty car park with just one old sedan sitting on the far end. Then an SUV—*Markus's*

SUV, she quickly realised—pulled into the spot directly opposite. She watched in silent confusion as her husband climbed out of the car and two figures rushed up behind him. There was a struggle. Her heart was in her throat as she saw her husband go limp and get carried over to the sedan. They put him in the boot.

The boot.

The sedan peeled away, and the video ended.

Elodie put the tablet down and stared at the detective.

"That video was taken at 8:47 am," he said. "We ran the plates. The car was stolen. As of this moment, we have no leads. Except that most likely these are the same people behind the delivery you reported to your house."

Hot, angry tears sprung up in Elodie's eyes. How could this have happened? Neural was meant to have state-of-the-art security.

"Mrs. Black," the detective said, surprisingly gently given his gung-ho appearance. "I need you to tell me if you've noticed anything else lately. Anything unusual. Anything at all, no matter how small."

Elodie tried to steady her breathing so she could think. Things had been strange for weeks, with all the media attention surrounding Markus's project.

"I've had messages on my socials," she said. "Hundreds of them. Death threats. Rape threats. You name it. Markus didn't say much, but I'm sure he got them as well."

Detective Burnett nodded. "We're reviewing those. Anything else?"

She didn't ask how they had access to her private messages.

"Nothing else that I noticed."

"Your husband didn't mention anything?"

Elodie shook her head. "No. If there was something, he probably wouldn't have wanted to worry me."

That was a problem, she realised. That her husband didn't feel he could tell her things. He probably thought she'd demand he stop his research.

The detective's phone buzzed. He stood, held up a hand as if to say *excuse me one moment*, and left the room.

Ears buzzing, Elodie watched the video again and again, searching for clues. It gave her nothing.

Markus, she thought wildly, as though she could reach him through telekinetic link. *Markus.*

Please come back to me.

If God would just bring him back safely, she'd be a better wife. She'd support him. She wouldn't get distracted by petty grievances. More than anything in the world, she wanted the chance to do that.

Please, God. If you would ever grant me one favour—let it be this. Give me my husband back.

She sat in silence for a long time.

Finally, she heard footsteps barreling down the hall. Detective Burnett burst through the door, still holding a phone to his ear. His face was flushed, and his eyebrows were raised so high she worried he might be about to have a stroke.

"Now," he barked. "Put him on *now.*"

His eyes met Elodie's, and he held out the phone. "I have your husband on the line."

* * *

After several hours of painstakingly detailed statements and a tsunami of paperwork, Elodie and Markus were finally allowed to leave the police station. It was dark when they got outside. Elodie's stomach growled. She realised, for the first time, that she hadn't eaten anything all day.

Markus reached for her hand as they walked toward the car. Elodie glanced at him out of the corner of her eye; her husband was smiling. That broad, easy, warm grin she loved most.

Elodie laughed. She felt lightheaded, and not just with hunger. It was almost as if the day had been a bad dream.

"Pizza?" Markus suggested as he unlocked the car. He slid into the driver's seat, and Elodie was grateful; she slumped into the passenger seat and closed her eyes.

"That sounds wonderful."

They drove in silence for a while, as the day's events replayed in Elodie's mind. There was just one thing that bothered her.

"Markus?"

He reached out to squeeze her shoulder. "Yes, love?"

"Don't you think it's weird that someone went to all that trouble of kidnapping you, only to let you escape by leaving a door unlocked? Don't you think that's weird? That they would be that careless? After all that effort to get past Neural's security?"

Her husband was silent for a while, making a few turns as they drew near their favourite pizzeria. He parked, and they sat under the glow of the neon sign through the windscreen.

"They didn't," he said at last. "I lied."

Elodie stared at him in stunned silence. Her throat was incredibly dry.

He stared back, gauging her reaction. "I saw them. I talked to them. They let me go."

"*What?*" Elodie sputtered. "You lied to the police? *Why?*"

Markus exhaled slowly. "Because they had a point."

"Explain," she growled, a little more savagely than she'd intended.

He smiled. "You know what you're always saying about me? Classic science geek, getting caught up in the ideas and not their real-world implications?"

"I'm not *always* saying that," Elodie protested. "Maybe once or twice."

Markus laughed. "Well, let's just say you might have more in common with our stalkers than you might think. You find the long term implications troubling from a religious perspective—they took issue from a socioeconomic perspective. Their concern is that immortality will create a superhuman race among the wealthy and leave the rest of humanity behind."

Elodie considered that for a moment. "Well, that could happen."

"Yes," Markus agreed. "It's something I should have thought about more. I guess I've always thought of myself as the lab guy, not the corporate guy. But I'll have to become more corporate if we want this technology to stay in the right hands."

"So," Elodie said, "they let you go because you convinced them you'd do that? Keep the technology safe?"

Markus smiled. He looked boyish, somehow, as he always did when something really excited him. "Better than that, and more ambitious. I convinced them I'd make it available for everyone."

"Everyone? Like everyone in the world?"

"Yep," he said, simply, and laughed again.

"A tall order," Elodie said.

"Very. But I think it's possible."

Elodie exhaled slowly. "Okay, then. No more threats?"

"Possibly. But not from them. Not if I keep to my word," Markus said.

"You'll find a way," she said, smiling at him. "You always do."

Her stomach growled again, and she grabbed her purse. "Ready to eat?"

"One more thing," Markus said, more hesitantly than before. "Though perhaps I should wait 'til you've had a glass of wine..."

Elodie laughed. "Tell me now. I can handle it. I mean, what could possibly be more wild than you getting into cahoots with your kidnappers?"

He smiled ruefully. "It is fairly wild. Perhaps I should wait until *I've* had a glass of wine."

She leaned over and kissed him on the cheek, breathing in his wonderful familiar scent. "Honestly, after today, you could tell me you want to move to Mars, and I'd probably agree."

Markus grinned, and kissed her in earnest. She put her arms around his neck, feeling the quickened beat of his heart.

"For a while there, I thought I'd never see you again," he whispered against her lips.

Elodie pressed her forehead against his. "Me, too."

"And it made me think... actually, I've been thinking this for a while..."

Elodie pulled back a little to look at him. His eyes glistened.

"I want us to have a baby," he whispered.

Elodie's blood ran cold. She recoiled into her seat, clutching her purse like a life raft.

"You know I can't," she said, almost choking.

"That's the thing," Markus said. "Everything's changing so fast. What was true three years ago isn't true anymore. I think maybe you *can*."

CHAPTER FIVE

UNTIL DEATH DO US PART

50 YEARS LATER

"Hey Google, what's the news?" Markus asked as he walked into the kitchen. The Home Helper knew his preference for a piping hot, single-origin latte upon rising; it switched its coffee component on and began to pour. An enticing aroma filled the kitchen.

Within one-tenth of a second, Google had scanned the entirety of the day's events and honed in on the headlines most likely to interest Markus.

"Globally, the IPCC has confirmed sea level stabilization at one meter above 1990 levels," the wall unit said in its soothing southern accent, personally selected by Markus. "Locally, there are protests underway in the X15 tunnel. Traffic is being re-routed. Therefore, you will need to leave eighteen minutes prior to your normal departure time in order to make your appointment."

Damnit. Elodie isn't even awake yet.

The soft, upbeat music in the kitchen shifted with his mood, to something a little more intense. "Sound off," he said, grabbing the latte. "Google, wake Elodie and turn off snooze mode."

Markus sat down to finish his coffee. He could hear Elodie's footsteps upstairs and the sound of water running through the pipes as she turned the shower on. In all the decades they'd been together, Elodie had never been a morning person, but he knew she was as excited about this day as he was. It was the culmination of his life's work.

Thus far, he corrected himself. If things went to plan, he would live a very long life indeed.

Before he had finished the latte, Elodie bounced down the stairs, still in her dressing gown. Right on cue, the Home Helper spat out two plates of eggs on toast.

Markus smiled to himself, recalling how creepy Elodie had found the presumption of their Home Helper when it was first installed. The Google algorithm which powered their appliances knew what Elodie and Markus liked better than they did. It knew everything from their food preferences to what their diet was deficient in, such as vitamin D when they weren't getting enough sun or iron and B vitamins when they were sluggish. The technology was so good, in fact, it predicted what each of them would enjoy eating within an accuracy percentile in the high nineties. On the exceptionally rare occasion the Home Helper failed, it wasn't worth the trouble of changing the settings and having to think about preparing their own breakfast.

Research showed time and again that a person could only make a limited number of calculated decisions in one day, so it was best to leave the mundane choices to the algorithm, saving their brain for the important decisions—the ones that, at least for now, should only be made by humans. For the sake of the freedom these conveniences allowed them, they had surrendered their privacy somewhere along the line, though neither Elodie nor Markus could recall exactly when it had happened. According to Elodie, it was an insidious process, but Markus saw how his wife constantly fought against the ever-changing world of technology. As far as Markus was concerned, the benefits were enormous and far outweighed any perceived consequences. In his view, their Home Helper was the world's best personal assistant, and it had only cost him his data.

Elodie looked up from her plate and smiled at him before she sliced open a perfectly poached egg. As he watched her eat, it struck Markus how lucky he was. At eighty-four years old, his wife was just as beautiful as the day he'd met her. Not just in the romantic sense of *still beautiful in my eyes*, but quite literally. She looked about thirty. Her body had been through a series of medical interventions, starting with a new heart when they learned she had the same cardiovascular disease which had killed her mother.

Methel had been alive on the third of July 2019, when *Health Day News* reported the first organ grown from stem cells, but she hadn't lived long enough to benefit from the technology. She'd died on the waiting list for a donor heart, like so many unfortunate potential organ recipients of that era.

By the time the weakening of Elodie's heart was first detected, they simply had to wait three months for a replacement to be grown in the lab. Though, in Markus's opinion, the greatest medical intervention his wife underwent was the one that allowed her to fall pregnant and become a mother to their daughter, Elexus, at the age of sixty five—a dream they had long ago given up hope of ever attaining.

"Big day," Elodie said, pulling him from his thoughts. "Nervous?"

Markus nodded. "I know I shouldn't be. Everything is in order, and theoretically, I can't foresee any issues whatsoever. We've covered all our bases. But yeah, I'd be lying if I said I wasn't a little nervous."

His wife smiled. "The final frontier. I'm proud of you."

Light footsteps clattered down the stairs, and Markus looked up in surprise. He couldn't remember the last time their daughter had risen before 9 am. He was even more taken aback to find her looking unusually well-groomed, wearing an elegant patterned tunic and slacks, with her long brown hair brushed and tied back. His heart seized gently—at nineteen, Elexus was almost entirely grown up. Soon she'd fly away into some new life.

Elodie's expression darkened as she took in the outfit. "*Where* are you going to wear such a sombre outfit?"

Elexus rolled her eyes and grabbed her coffee from the Home Helper. "Honestly, Mother, you must be the only parent in history to complain that her daughter's outfits are too modest."

Markus sighed internally and busied himself with consuming his breakfast. He'd long since stopped intervening in their mother-daughter disputes.

"You're going to do something with *them*," Elodie accused. "As if you didn't spend enough time there over the weekend. And what's this 'mother' business? I thought these Eastern religions taught you to be more respectful to your parents."

Their daughter scowled. Markus caught her sneaking a glance in his direction as if pleading with him to intervene. His heart sank: there was nothing he hated more than getting in the middle of an argument between the two loves of his life, and he again lowered his gaze to his plate.

"*Mother* is perfectly respectful," Elexus said sullenly.

"You make the word *mother* sound derogatory, which I know you do on purpose. You were barely home on Easter. You're rejecting everything we taught you—all the values of this family. You think that's respect?" Elodie demanded, her eyes shining.

Markus couldn't bear this any longer. "Enough. We're glad you're exploring different ideologies, sweetheart; there's nothing wrong with that. We just want to understand. Perhaps you could take us to the mosque tomorrow? You can tell us what you see in this faith, and we'll listen."

Pouring her coffee into a travel cup, Elexus did not respond. Then she gave a slight, perfunctory nod. For a brief, revealing moment, he saw the truth in his daughter's eyes—she still cared what her parents thought.

Markus stood up and pulled Elexus into a tight hug. His daughter wrapped her arms around him, like she had when she was little, and gave him a squeeze before rushing out the door. When he turned back to Elodie, his wife was shaking her head.

"If you think," she said, "I can sit down and listen to her preach to us about that religion, you overestimate me."

Markus reached across the counter and touched her hand. "No, sweetheart, I think you underestimate yourself. Elexus isn't a child anymore, and whether you like it or not, she has her own opinions, many of which don't line up with yours or mine. That doesn't make them any less valid. Fighting it will only push her away. Do you really want that?"

Elodie sighed. Markus sensed he might be winning her over.

"There's nothing to say she won't return to your church in time, but it's important for Elexus to find her own way. We just need to shut up and listen," he added.

"Apologies for the interjection," the Home Helper piped up. "Your car will arrive in five minutes."

Elodie shot upstairs to get dressed, and Markus tried to put the unpleasantness out of his mind. He landed back on something Elodie had said earlier: *the final frontier.* An apt expression. These days, everything could be replaced or renewed—except the brain. None of these miraculous interventions came cheap. Sometimes Markus wasn't sure if he should be glad of the updates so that he could keep working, or glad he could keep working to afford the updates. But as long as their brains stayed sharp, it wasn't a problem: he and Elodie should be able to keep working and getting updates indefinitely.

Even with an eternally youthful body to support it, the human brain couldn't function forever. Many of Markus's older colleagues at Neural had fallen prey to some form of dementia. It didn't matter what precautions they took; eventually the brain failed. It was only a matter of time before the same fate befell him or Elodie... unless, of course, his project was successful.

He could see the marketing already: *Brain uploading. The final frontier.*

* * *

Settling into the back seat of the self-driving car, Elodie reached out and slipped her hand into Markus's. She hoped she looked more relaxed than she felt because, as much as Elodie hated to admit it, she was nervous, too. Confident though she was in her husband's research, there were so many things that could go wrong. It was all fresh in her mind as they had stayed up all night discussing them.

Of all the possibilities, Elodie thought the worst would be if something corrupted the data, either during the upload or the download. Markus assured her the risk of such an incident was miniscule, but she was not completely reassured. She had been unable to get to sleep for thinking about it; how even a small error could have massive consequences to the character of a person. It could change who they were.

What if I uploaded my mind, and something happened to me, and Markus or Elexus brought me back only to find that I was no longer the same person as before? It wouldn't matter if it was something subtle or obvious. I still wouldn't be me anymore, not really. Or what if something happened to Markus, and I had to download him only to find myself married to a stranger?

Elodie couldn't think of anything more devastating and swallowed thickly as she forced the thought from her mind— but not before Markus noticed.

"What are you worrying about?" he asked, gently squeezing her hand.

She shrugged, avoiding his gaze. "Just about your project."

"Oh?" he prompted.

"I was thinking about what makes us who we are. You know, our little quirks and things that make us individuals. I mean,

I know that everyone changes over time, and that's perfectly normal. But if that change happened all at once..."

"Ah." He nodded slowly. "You're worried about corruption."

Elodie smiled wryly at her husband. After all their decades together, it was like he could read her mind. Then her smile faded as she wondered if that was something else that could be lost with a download.

What if we were no longer in sync as a couple? It would feel like learning to walk again.

"I thought I said last night that it was only a minor risk. It's really nothing for you to worry about," Markus continued.

"I know you did, and I know you think I'm being irrational. I also know you've got safeguards in place to prevent something like that from happening. It's just the idea of it, you know? To come back as something less than you were could be worse than death."

Markus shifted in his seat so he could face her better. "You don't have to do this with me if you don't want to. I'll understand. Perhaps it was selfish to ask this of you..."

"Don't be silly! Of course I want to be by your side and do this together. You've worked so hard for this, and for so long. I'm proud of you, but I'm also scared... for us."

"I understand that. I'm just saying it's not too late for you to change your mind."

Elodie laughed, but it sounded high-pitched and strained. "No, I'm just being morbid. We've talked this over a thousand times; I want to do it. Let's talk about something else."

Markus nodded. "How about some tunes?" He leaned forward slightly, "Google, play Led Zeppelin's greatest hits." He leaned back again as the music started, and Elodie felt herself relax alongside him as she focused on the lyrics instead of her own thoughts.

They rode in silence for a while before the car's AI spoke: "Please be advised we are diverting over the X15 to avoid the protest taking place in the tunnel."

"Thank you," Markus said with a sigh.

"Protest? What about this time?" Elodie asked.

"Let's find out," Markus said. "Hey Google, provide a news update on the tunnel protest."

Immediately, the news update sounded through the car.

"Thousands of anti-immigrant protesters have swarmed the X15 this morning, protesting the recent influx of climate refugees into the country. Despite the government claiming they were winning the war against climate change, for populations in low-lying areas throughout the world, their success is too little too late. With many countries struggling under the strain of providing for these climate refugees, anti-immigrant sentiment is at a fever pitch..."

"News off," Elodie said firmly as she scowled.

"I'm sorry, sweetheart," Markus said softly.

Elodie didn't respond. She couldn't help but take the news personally. Her whole career had been spent trying to prevent these exact outcomes.

"Are you okay?" Markus asked.

"Not entirely," Elodie admitted, "but I don't want to focus on the negatives right now. Don't you think it's great what Dubai's done?"

Markus grinned. "Where did that come from?"

"I have no idea. It was the first thing that came into my head. So?"

"What is there to say about using cheap foreign labour to build a nation?"

Elodie laughed, despite herself. "*No*. I mean more recently. Seems like they've managed to put an end to the 'us and them' mentality for just 'us', as in mankind. Every other country is still set on restricting other people and cultures from infiltrating their own."

"I don't see that changing any time soon, despite what Dubai has achieved." He patted her hand. "Though there are several prophecies that speak of a unified world. The Jewish Torah speaks of the end times when there will be no jealousy or rivalry... and the Zoroastrians predict a time when all humanity will speak a single language and belong to a single nation with no borders."

Elodie suppressed a groan; decades together and Markus still insisted on quoting from religions he didn't believe in. Though now was not the time for that argument.

"Everyone's so afraid of losing their way of life," she pressed, "but Dubai put their culture and ideals at risk by opening the floodgates, allowing foreign nationals to enter and help build a new country—and they did! They built a whole new culture that's unique to Dubai. They may have lost their old one, but all cultures die eventually. None of the cultures we have today are truly ancient. France today is completely different to France a hundred years ago, and it's probably better."

"That all depends on who you talk to..." Markus said, but Elodie ignored him.

"I think that's what will happen everywhere, eventually. Cultures are fluid, and I honestly believe, one day, there will no longer be 'us and them'. I think there will be just 'us'. Dubai has shown us it's possible."

"Or," Markus said playfully, "what if it's literally just us? What if everyone else dies in a fiery Armageddon, but we are spared because our minds will be backed up?"

Elodie rolled her eyes. "Is there no subject which you can't turn back to brain uploading?"

"Doubt it." Markus grinned.

"I'm serious. If humans do end up living forever, it's more important than ever for us to solve this problem. We can't stay stuck in the past. I think we'll have to embrace the Dubai model; make a world based on *us*. No more what's best for our country to the detriment of other countries. We need to stop fearing asylum-seekers and wrongly believing 'they' may reduce 'our' standard of living. I like to think that one day all of humanity will be working together for the good of 'us' as a species as opposed to 'us', our family, city, religion or country."

Elodie was grateful to see Markus's expression turn serious. "I've always loved what a big, beautiful heart you have, darling. I hope you're right. I can't wait to share eternity with you and see that world come about."

Their car stopped; they'd arrived at Neural headquarters, exactly as the clock flicked over to 8:00 am. Elodie's stomach clenched fiercely, and despite all her instincts, she took Markus's hand and allowed him to lead her from the car.

* * *

Markus woke up feeling as if he had downed a bottle of tequila the night before. As he opened his eyes, the fluorescent lighting seemed to tunnel painfully into his brain. Someone was hovering to his left, as the smell of perfume drifted towards him.

Elodie.

He reached up for her hand and was comforted by the familiar warmth of her skin, sending a surge of relief coursing through him.

"What time is it?" he asked.

"6:07 pm," Elodie said as she stroked his hair back from his face.

"Drew?" Markus called out, though he couldn't see his assistant anywhere. "Let's run a back test on the data and complete the defrag."

"Only you would jump straight back into work mode after having your brain uploaded," Elodie said affectionately.

"Hmm," Markus said. "I need a drink of water."

Within seconds, an assistant in a white lab coat—Fran, he thought her name was—appeared at his other side, handing him a paper cup while simultaneously raising the bed so that Markus could sit up. He sipped the water gratefully as the fog cleared a little. "I want to see the readings."

"Babe, maybe give yourself the chance to recover fully first..." Elodie suggested.

"Now, please," he said to Fran before turning to his wife. She looked pale and tired, perched on the edge of her own bed in a hospital-style gown. He felt a pang of guilt. "I'm fine, really. Just eager to see the results."

Elodie nodded, sighing, and slumped against her pillows. Drew finally appeared, wheeling over a laptop on a hospital table and positioning it over his mattress. Taking a deep breath, Markus tapped away as streams of data appeared on the screen. He'd never felt so nervous in all his long life. Finally, he looked up at his wife and grinned.

"It *worked*, babe. The scans are complete! My backup is being saved to the cloud as we speak."

"That's amazing," she said, pressing her hands to her face before jumping up and throwing her arms around him. "Congratulations! I am so proud of you!"

"Thank you, love. I feel like I need to pinch myself."

"Does this mean we can go home?" Elodie asked. "It's been such a long day."

"Soon," he promised. "Let me just finish my final checks, and then we can go home and celebrate."

Elodie slumped back into a chair with a sigh. Markus felt another stab of guilt; it had been a big day for both of them, and it must have been stressful for Elodie to regain consciousness first and have to wait for him to do so.

"You're right," he said. "It's enough to know the upload was successful. Anything else can wait—at least until tomorrow." He grinned.

Elodie smiled back as she stood and scooped up her handbag. "Good. I just want to get home and have a hot shower."

Markus allowed her to help him get changed. Elodie insisted on holding his arm as she guided him out of the lab and to the elevator, not letting go even as they rode it down to the lobby, or when they stepped out of the facility as their car pulled up. Only once he was seated in the back did Elodie let go of his hand.

"The tunnel protest should be over by now, don't you think?" Elodie said as she closed the door behind her.

"Your guess is as good as mine. What's the update, Google?" Markus asked.

"Anti-refugee protests resolved around 10:15 am local time. There is minor congestion through the tunnels. You will be home in twelve minutes."

"Thank you," Markus said, as he leaned back against the seat and turned to his wife. She returned his smile before gazing out the window, and as he continued to watch her, Markus felt grateful she'd convinced him to leave. He was far more tired than he originally thought.

They rode in silence at first, each of them lost in their own thoughts, before Elodie reached for his hand.

"Drink?"

Markus laughed. "Probably inadvisable, given the anesthesia, but why not? We have a lot to celebrate."

He reached into the minibar and cracked open two cans of premixed gin and tonic.

His eyes met hers as he handed her the drink. Markus felt struck by her beauty, as he often did, yet despite her ageless features, her eyes gave away the number of decades she had been alive.

"I think I'll come with you tomorrow," she said suddenly. "Perhaps you're right. I need to let Elexus make her own choices."

"That is a wonderful idea, sweetheart. I promise you won't regret it, and I know our daughter will appreciate it. Cheers." Markus held his drink out to his wife, but before they could connect, their faces were brightly illuminated by the lights of an approaching vehicle and the car exploded. He felt his body lurch forward, and the last thing he saw was glass falling around him like rain.

CHAPTER SIX

THE END OF MATERIALISM

Elodie blinked slowly and groaned. She looked out the window and couldn't make sense of what she saw: an upside-down world, with glass scattered across the asphalt like stars in the night sky, and like a moon, one headlight of a truck shone through the steam roiling out of its front grill. Her eyes widened as she spotted Markus sprawled on the ground some distance away. One of his arms was positioned at an unnatural angle. Something ran down his face, and it took her a moment to realise it was blood. More than just a trickle. A pool of it was spreading outward from beneath his head. Her breaths came in short, sharp sobs as she fought against her seatbelt in her hurry to reach him.

"Calling emergency services," the car's AI said in her calm British accent. "Your ambulance will arrive in six minutes."

Too long, Elodie thought wildly. *God help us, please!*

She looked out again to where Markus lay in the street. There weren't many lights or people in this part of town; half the block had been closed down and fenced off for a new development, and most of the remaining shops were shut. If there was anyone around, no one came to help. All she could see, in the dim light, was Markus and the blood. *Oh, God, all that blood.*

Markus never wore his seatbelt, and Elodie had stopped nagging him about it years ago. People rarely bothered these days, with the automation of vehicles bringing crash statistics close to nil. Elodie only used hers as a kind of superstitious ritual, much to Markus's amusement.

Markus...

Wincing, Elodie looked around, trying to work out how to free herself. There was an inflated airbag pressed against her chest. She raised one arm overhead to brace herself against the ceiling, taking the weight off the seatbelt long enough to release the buckle. The airbag cushioned her fall.

Move! Elodie crawled out through the shattered rear windscreen, only dimly registering the glass biting into her forearms. Staggering, she made her way to Markus before collapsing at his side. With her left hand, she pressed her fingers to the side of his neck. She could feel a pulse, but it was faint.

She wouldn't take her eyes off him. Irrationally, she told herself that if she didn't look away, he wouldn't die; it would be impossible to *see Markus die*. He, who had chatted her up at university with his irrepressible grin. He, who had been there ever since, when she graduated and got her first job and had their daughter and lost her mother. Her husband had his faults, but he was nothing if not dependable. Markus was the love of her life, and he would not die before her very eyes. God wouldn't allow it.

"Markus, sweetheart, I'm here! Just hang in there. The ambulance is on its way. Just hang in there."

Don't leave me.

After a lifetime of talking and listening, and sometimes blocking him out, there was so much more she wanted to say—a million tiny things that only Markus would understand. Even the freak nature of their accident. The authorities would investigate how such a glitch had occurred. Was it a technical fault, or something more sinister, like a cyber hijacking in protest of his work?

Not Markus, though. He would ask different questions: was his fate already determined by previously existing causes? If he was going to meet God, whose God would it turn out to be?

Flashing red and blue lights pulled Elodie from her trance, and she took her eyes off her husband just long enough to see an ambulance pull up. Two paramedics jumped out, a man and a woman. Elodie watched numbly as they raced over and checked Markus's pulse.

"It's thready," the woman said to her partner.

"What does that mean?" Elodie demanded. Her voice came out as a barely audible croak. She tried again, louder: "What are you doing to my husband?"

"Ma'am, are you hurt? Can you stand up for me?" the male paramedic asked, as though he didn't hear her question. He helped her to her feet before guiding her over to the trolley. Elodie tried to fight against him as he gently pushed her shoulders down, but she was weaker than she realised, and her body put up little resistance despite her mind screaming at her to return to her husband. The paramedic placed an oxygen mask over her face before dashing back to his partner, who was at Markus's side.

Where I should be.

Her grip on consciousness was weakening, but Elodie fought as hard as she could; if Markus thought she'd gone, he might not fight as hard to hang on, and she couldn't bear that thought. After what felt like an eternity, the paramedics wheeled him into the back of the ambulance beside her. The fluorescent lights made him appear ghostly pale. As she tried to reach out for him with her left hand, Elodie lost her fight and passed out.

* * *

Elodie had no concept of how much time had passed since they had arrived at the hospital. She'd regained consciousness in a haze of strong painkillers. The nurse told her that they hadn't been able to contact Elexus. Elodie called three times with no answer. Finally, she sent the message she didn't want to send.

We had a car crash. I'm okay, but Dad is in a bad way. Get to the hospital as soon as you can.

Finally, she was permitted to see Markus, but nothing could have prepared her for the sight of him. He looked small and frail in the hospital bed, hooked up to expensive-looking machines. Tubes snaked into his nose, mouth and hands. The nurse praised the handiwork of the doctor who had expertly closed the wound on his head—*for the time being.*

"What does that mean?" Elodie had asked, only to be told the doctor would be with her soon to explain.

That was over an hour ago, and no one had come.

Elodie carefully grasped Markus's hand. Bowing her head, she prayed she would have better news by the time her daughter called back.

The sound of shoes squeaking against the linoleum floor pulled Elodie from her prayers, and she looked up hopefully, her heart sinking as she watched the same nurse approach her husband. She looked terribly young, with her brown hair tied up in a perky ponytail. It was difficult to tell, these days, but all the nurses Elodie had seen looked like they couldn't be older than twenty five.

Why is this hospital staffed by children? she screamed internally, knowing the answer that personal care jobs were highly demanding and chronically underpaid.

"I'm just going to check his vitals, and then we're running further tests. The doctor shouldn't be long," the nurse said kindly, which only made Elodie want to scream out loud. Instead, she nodded curtly and squeezed her hands together in such tight fists she could feel her fingernails cutting into her palms.

"Please," Elodie asked, unable to stop her voice from shaking. "Please tell me what you can. Anything at all."

The young nurse sighed. Elodie wished she hadn't spoken; the nurse's eyes told her more than words could. She swallowed thickly, as though it could stop the panic rising within her chest.

"Your husband has a severe brain injury, a broken arm and collarbone, a collapsed lung, several skull fractures, a broken leg, and what looks like a broken spine. We need the swelling to subside before we can know for sure," the young woman said gently. "The machine is keeping him alive, technically, helping him breathe. We'll be taking him for more scans soon, which will be followed by further surgery. But you should prepare yourself. The brain is the one thing we can't necessarily fix. There's a chance your husband cannot be saved. I'm very sorry. I have to take him now, and I'm afraid you can't come."

Kicking the brakes off the bed, the nurse wheeled him out into the hall, leaving Elodie to stare after them long after they'd disappeared.

The buzzing of her phone snapped her out of it, and as she scurried to her feet, Elodie was relieved to see it was Elexus.

"Sweetheart…"

"How bad is it?" Elexus asked in a rush, her panic evident, "Is he going to die?"

"No, sweetheart, of course not," Elodie replied.

She fought a wave of panic; what if something changed while Markus was out of her sight?

He couldn't die. She believed it with every fibre of her being.

And yet, during the second surgery, he did.

* * *

Around 7 am, after two hours' fitful sleep, Elodie woke up in a world that was alien to her. She was home, in her own bed, but Markus was not there. For the first time in decades, she was alone. It still felt like a dream, the very worst kind, and yet she knew that it wasn't. Markus had *died.* Her husband, the love of her life, lay on a steel table in the Saint Peter's Hospital morgue while her clothes, crumpled on the bedroom floor, were stained with his blood. Even though she could see the evidence, even though she remembered every excruciating detail, the idea was impossible to wrap her head around. It was surreal.

But another idea had surfaced as she drifted between sleep and waking. She'd been in such terror all night that she had forgotten something crucially important. Perhaps God was watching over her, after all; he'd let the unthinkable happen but at the kindest possible moment.

Right now, a perfect backup of her husband was stored at Neural headquarters.

She could bring Markus back.

CHAPTER SEVEN

WHY HAST THOU FORSAKEN ME?

Elodie arrived at Neural at 7:55 am, five minutes before the automatic sliding doors would unlock. The imposing glass-and-steel facade of the Neural building towered eighteen storeys overhead. She had never taken the time to really look at it before; she'd always just walked straight inside with Markus, her thoughts elsewhere. Yet, now that Markus was gone, she finally admired the truly impressive company he had helped grow into the most successful and prestigious in its field. Markus had made many sacrifices over the decades for the sake of Neural's success, though she had never appreciated the reasons why until now.

She wished she had told him earlier how proud she was of his achievements.

You will tell him, she promised herself. *Soon.*

Scanning the faces of the employees streaming off the company shuttle, Elodie felt a little bit dizzy. The night had been long, and she hadn't eaten since the eggs with Markus at breakfast yesterday. But her stomach was clenched like a fist. She couldn't eat until she'd accomplished what she came here to do.

A familiar face came off the shuttle: Costa, Markus's lead assistant, a distinctive-looking young man with dark hair and olive skin which hinted at Greek heritage. She darted towards him, pushing past the slow stream of employees heading for the food hall. Costa seemed more purposeful than most; he was walking fast, heading straight for the elevator. Elodie caught up with him just as the doors sprang open.

He jumped and turned around, his eyes wide before recognition set in. "Mrs. Black! Ah… can I help you?"

"I hope so," Elodie said fervently. They stepped into the elevator and Costa pressed the button for the seventh floor.

She drew in a deep breath. "Markus… my husband…"

Now, he looked at her with obvious unease.

"… he died," she finished, feeling faint. "We got in an accident and he died."

The elevator spun a little; the young man grabbed her arm as if to steady her. "Mrs. Black, I—"

"Please call me Elodie," she managed.

"Elodie," he said, looking pale underneath his tan. "I am… so very sorry for your loss. Markus was a magnificent man. A genius."

Elodie nodded absently. The elevator doors sprang open; Costa kept hold of her arm, leading her past the lab and into his small office. He shut the door and gestured for her to sit, but they both remained standing.

"I appreciate you coming all this way to tell me, but I'm assuming there's a reason you're here in person?" Costa asked.

Elodie nodded slowly, forcing herself to meet his gaze. "I want to know," she said carefully, "what it will take to use my husband's backup. I'm aware that you don't have the hardware developed to house it in conscious form—yet. I'm asking you what it will take. How far off is that project from completion? Who's working on it, and how much money is needed? I'm a researcher myself, and I want to do whatever I can to expedite the process."

Costa exhaled deeply. "Mrs. Black..."

She looked at him with steely determination. *Mrs. Black* was not an answer. Was he about to patronise her?

"The backup didn't work."

His words registered like a sucker punch to her gut.

"That's not right," she snapped. "I was there yesterday. The backup was successful. Markus said everything went perfectly. *Perfectly.* There is no way he would miss an error if there was one. There is no way he would have *left* if there was a problem."

When Costa finally raised his head, he gazed at her with wide-eyed horror, like a kid caught out in an illicit act. "Mrs. Black, I mean Elodie, the scan itself worked. It *was* perfect. But during the process of converting the upload of data into a backup, the procedure was not completed."

"I don't understand."

"Well, during the process of saving Markus's data to our servers, the upload stalled. I saw the notification shortly after you left. I was certain there would be a simple solution, and I sent Markus a message to call me. When he didn't, I assumed that he wasn't concerned—he designed the system after all—and that he would look into it when he got back to the lab.

So, the upload timed out and I went home. I didn't think he could possibly..."

Die. The word hung in the air unsaid.

Elodie swallowed. Her mouth was very dry, and the room was spinning again. Dark clouds crept in from the edge of her vision. For a brief, confusing moment she couldn't see anything, despite having her eyes wide open. Then, mercifully, everything went blank.

* * *

Elodie had never been suicidal, but in the days that followed Costa's news she did wonder if she'd lived long enough. Elexus had finally called back to say she was staying at a friend's house for a while; Elodie begged her to come home, but Elexus had screamed, hung up, and been unreachable ever since.

With only herself for company, Elodie just lay on the bed, her thoughts circling over and over those last moments with Markus in the lab. He'd wanted to keep working, but *she'd* wanted to go home, and she hadn't bothered to hide her feelings. It was a small moment of selfishness in the bigger picture of a day where she'd supported her husband unconditionally. Despite her reservations, she'd agreed to do the backup. She'd been perfectly willing to be a guinea pig to support Markus's ambitions. She'd taken time off work and woken up much earlier than usual to be at the lab on time. But none of that mattered. Everything came down to another moment, where she'd demanded to go home and put Markus in the path of the truck.

In case she could ever consider forgiving herself for her role in her husband's death, there was also the fact that she'd cost him eternal life. Costa had been reluctant to confirm it, but Elodie quickly inferred that Markus's upload would likely have been successful if he had stayed back to follow the protocol. Meanwhile, *Elodie's* upload had finished without a hitch. *Elodie* was preserved forever, in perfect detail, on a server at Neural.

Feeling as though her limbs were filled with lead, she dragged herself off the bed and into the shower, where she stood directly beneath the hot torrent of water. She'd always loved to luxuriate under the hot water, but today she felt nothing but pain.

Markus had designed the bathroom especially to her tastes, with a double showerhead and steam setting. It used to be her happy place, but now it was just another reminder of how she'd taken him for granted. She slumped against the shower screen and slammed her open palm against the glass, screaming in agony. Part of her hoped the glass would shatter, but it didn't, of course; it was safety glass, made to withstand the weight of a falling human and then some—she recalled Markus telling her so. Regardless, she slammed it again and was mildly gratified by the pain.

It would be easier if she could cry, but the tears wouldn't come. Elodie didn't believe she deserved the relief they might provide. There was only the impenetrable numbness that not even Elexus could touch, had she wanted to. In truth, she was glad her daughter had decided to stay with her friends, as much as she wanted her close. Having to look at her, and her resemblance to Markus, to witness her daughter's pain and grief, would only make the guilt more unbearable.

Having gone through the motions of washing her hair, she towelled herself off and went back to bed. The Home Helper was disabled, ever since she'd informed Elodie that Markus's funeral was arranged for 4 pm tomorrow. The Home Helper had it all covered: bookings, payments, the guest list, an appropriate array of photos, a carefully analysed selection of songs from her husband's favourite playlists. She knew she ought to be grateful. Instead, she'd screamed at it to "*die* until further notice".

Sounds tempting, she thought. But no—she didn't exactly want to die. But she didn't want to live either. Not with the knowledge that she had cost Markus his eternity.

* * *

She was still in bed, her head on a wet pillow, when the doorbell rang. *Dear Lord God, please no*, she mouthed silently. The doorbell rang again. Next, a fist hammered on the door.

Then, as she heard the *beep* of their security system disarming, her stomach clenched.

"Welcome, Archer," the system announced.

Elodie sat bolt upright and searched frantically for her robe. She located it within the duvet, pulling it on just as Archer's footsteps thundered up the stairs.

There was a pause before he knocked politely on the bedroom door.

"Bit late for that, don't you think?" Elodie called out. "I just want to be left alone to gather my strength for tomorrow. Is that too much to ask?"

The door swung open, revealing Archer hovering upon the threshold to her room. He looked almost exactly the same as when they first met fifty-two years ago; a slightly different cut to the suit, in line with the current fashion, but the same youthful face, the same perfectly coiffed hair and expensive aura. Some things would never change.

Elodie's mind drifted for a moment as she considered how her friendship with Archer had endured, despite meeting him through Kayla, who she'd inevitably fallen out with. Though, after five decades, Elodie could barely remember the specifics. Archer and Kayla broke up, and Archer stuck around. She had come to trust him like a brother. He would even check in on the house when Elodie and Markus took trips away, which was why he had security access. She hadn't bothered to revoke it after their last holiday—an oversight she now regretted.

"My God," he said softly. "You look…"

Elodie almost snarled. "What? Not glamorous enough for you? Forgive me. Had I known you were coming, I'd have blow-dried my hair."

She wouldn't have, of course. She'd have revoked his security access.

He shook his head. "Not so. I was going to say that you look like you're not sleeping."

Something about his tone took her off guard. He wasn't judging her.

The compassion broke her; at long last, she started crying—huge, wracking, ugly sobbing. Her grief intensified, but at the same time, it felt like a weight being lifted. She fell back onto the bed, clutching a pillow as she howled like a wounded animal, rocking back and forth. Elodie was only mildly aware that Archer still hovered in the doorway, clearly uncomfortable but determined to stay. Yet, now that she'd started, it felt impossible to stop.

Once her keening subsided, Archer strode over to the wardrobe and flung it open. He pulled out the closest thing to hand, the burgundy dress she had worn to church last Sunday.

He threw it on the bed. "Put that on and get your hair dry. I'm taking you out for food."

Elodie stared at him blankly.

"You've turned your Home Helper off, right? So there's no food in the house."

She nodded.

"Then we're going out. Nothing fancy. Chuck the dress on and be downstairs in five minutes."

To her own surprise, Elodie got dressed, dried her hair and put shoes on, as if on autopilot. She didn't have the will to argue. And—more surprising still—she realised she actually was famished.

Four days of not eating had taken their toll. The dress that had fit on Sunday was now loose, and her legs trembled slightly as she walked downstairs. As much as she hated to admit it, it felt good to be up, moving, and wearing something other than her robe.

"Where are we going?" she asked Archer, who was waiting patiently in the kitchen, lounging at the breakfast bar. Her heart seized painfully at the sight of another man in Markus's customary position—her husband would never eat breakfast there again.

Your fault, she reminded herself. *Completely your fault.*

Archer sprung up as though he'd read her mind, ushering her down the hallway and out the front door before she could reconsider the outing. "As I said, nothing fancy. I was thinking the noodle house on the corner. Thought you might enjoy a walk."

So, they didn't have to take an autocar. *Thank God for that.*

They walked in silence, their eyes on the ground, only occasionally looking up to check their location. The street buzzed with life; it was the tail end of rush hour, so a stream of cars whirred by, some pulling up in front of the luxury apartments lining her street. Elodie kept her head down until they reached the restaurant, hoping desperately she wouldn't run into anyone she knew. Archer was bad enough; she definitely couldn't bear small talk from neighbours and listen to their hollow condolences before they continued to whisper about how dreadful she looked the moment her back was turned.

How do people survive this kind of loss?

Elodie thought of all the people she'd known over the decades who had lost husbands and wives and children. She realised that, for all her Catholic beliefs, she had not shown them nearly enough compassion; she had only given a thinly-veiled empathy at best, the kind that comes from someone who doesn't think they will ever be touched with the same darkness and sorrow.

The restaurant was crowded, humming with music, conversation and the chiming of cutlery. Rich smells of soup and sizzling hotplate dishes filled the air. The maître d' was an elegant woman in traditional Chinese dress. Archer nodded to her, and Elodie recognised her smile as registering a substantial digital tip.

They were guided at once to one of the best seats in the restaurant, a private booth overlooking the street. Elodie slumped onto the padded seat while Archer rattled off an order. Finally, once the waiter left, he looked her in the eye.

"I don't know anything about what you're going through," he admitted, looking almost bashful. "I've been lucky; I've never lost anyone."

Elodie nodded. "With enough money and a bit more luck, perhaps you'll never have to."

Ignoring the jibe, Archer continued, "He was still working on that immortality thing, wasn't he? I'm sorry he didn't finish it."

Elodie breathed out slowly and gritted her teeth in an attempt to keep from crying. "He did finish it."

Archer went very pale. "You mean... is *he...?*"

"No," she whispered. "No, his upload didn't work. But his staff have told me that mine did."

She slumped forward onto the table and buried her face in her hands. A waiter appeared with their appetisers and drinks. Taking in her body language, he laid the food down and disappeared without a word.

Archer leaned forward to talk in a whisper. "You're... backed up on a server somewhere? Seriously? They're sure?"

Elodie glared at him through her fingers. "They're sure. The wrong upload worked, and it worked perfectly. Apparently, I'm the first immortal human. I wish I could convince them to delete it and let me die. I don't want to live forever. I want to go to Heaven, and see Markus, and tell him..."

She began to choke with the effort it took her to keep from sobbing. With a stricken expression, Archer poured her a cold glass of water. She took a sip, but it barely eased the strained feeling in her throat.

"I never loved him enough," she choked out. "I realise that now. All these years, through everything, I took him so much for granted, Archer. I treated him the way Mum treated Dad. Not really listening most of the time. Acting like being there and providing for the family was all he was good for. But I miss him so much. I'll never forgive myself for any of this. I finally want to talk to him, really talk to him, more than *anything*, and he's not here. I'll never talk to him again. Unless I die and see him in Heaven."

"For what it's worth," Archer said, "I think you will be happy again. We don't share the same faith anymore, but some things are common to all religions. You believe in Heaven and the immortal soul; I believe in the cycle of samsara and rebirth. But the end is not so different."

After Kayla, Archer had dated a glamorous blonde Buddhist. The woman hadn't stuck, but to everyone's surprise, her penchant for yoga and meditation had. He still took his mother to church on Sundays but had been a practising Buddhist for decades.

Elodie forced herself to take an egg roll and start chewing while Archer carried on. "Perhaps it is for the best that Markus's upload didn't work. You've always struggled with the thought of yourself transcending to an eternal life through your religion while Markus stayed grounded to this world through his tech. This way, maybe you will be together again one day."

"You're missing the point, Archer. It doesn't matter what I want. *Markus* wanted it, and now because of me, he can't have it."

"I honestly can't wrap my head around the backup thing," Archer confessed as he reached for another egg roll. "It might be a copy of you, but it's not really you, is it? I mean, they could download that data to an android right now, who'd go on living under the illusion that it's you, and theoretically you'd be none the wiser."

"No, they couldn't," Elodie said, swallowing the egg roll with some effort. "They're not able to produce a synthetic brain that could house human consciousnesses. Yet."

He waved her off as though the technology was unimportant. "I mean theoretically. If they could make such a brain, they could download your data and create a new being that is merely under the *illusion* that it's you. Though really, we're all in that boat. We're all—"

"Suffering under the illusion of self," Elodie finished for him, sighing. Archer's Buddhist rhetoric had grown repetitive over the years, though she appreciated his current train of thought. Under the present circumstances, it would be a relief to think that the entity she thought of as *Elodie Black* was an illusion. She didn't want to be this grief-stricken, guilty woman with no redemption in sight.

"Yes," Archer said in a serious tone of voice. "Ultimately, I don't think it matters whether the backup is really you or not. I don't buy into that distinction, since we're all made of the same stuff, and we'll end up as one in Nirvana, if you follow the Buddhist line of thinking. But surely it's not a problem from the Christian perspective either? I don't think the backup could have stolen your soul. Either your soul will meet Markus's in Heaven or your individual consciousness will become one with his as a pure collective consciousness, liberated from desire and suffering. According to either belief system, I think you'll find peace."

Elodie found herself blinking back tears. More food arrived: chicken noodle soup, fried lotus flowers, barbecue pork, rice, and small glasses of *baijiu*, the traditional Chinese liquor. Despite the relatively casual style of the restaurant, she knew that the meat must be expensive, so she forced herself to keep eating.

"Honestly," she admitted, "I'm not sure what to believe anymore. All my life, I thought God was looking after me. I even thought so the night of the accident—I figured that if God had to take Markus, he must have waited until after the backup, so I wouldn't have to live without him. I thought things made *sense*. But nothing does."

Archer was nodding. "Forgive me for saying this; I know Buddhism isn't your thing. But that feeling, that's what got me started on this path. It helps, sometimes, to try to accept that attachment to any particular outcome brings suffering. We can't control what happens. Maybe one day we'll know more and be able to understand. Until then," he raised his glass, "there's acceptance and *baijiu*."

"And therapy," Elodie said, taking her shot of liquor. "I think I'm going to start."

* * *

Therapy, she reflected after Archer saw her home, could be her salvation. It would be good to feel like someone was actually listening. But perhaps the therapist could also help her become a different person: a better version of herself who wouldn't keep making the same mistakes.

In a way, this was also her assurance that the backup hadn't captured her soul. The backup was static, whereas *she* could change. In fact, if she put her mind to it, she could become an entirely new person.

She sat up half the night, thinking. Could the backup of Markus have captured his soul, or was it merely a snapshot in time? Could she, through therapy, become a different person, a better person? Yes, she decided, the backup, if brought back, would have made the same decisions in the future as the original Markus would have made. But his soul... she couldn't decide.

At 2 am, she rebooted the Home Helper and asked her to book the best therapist in the city.

"Did you say *therapist?*" it queried politely. She did that when a person mumbled, or when they acted in ways the algorithm didn't anticipate.

Elodie felt a small flush of pleasure. If she was able to surprise the Home Helper, perhaps the transformation was already underway.

With that small mission accomplished, all the fatigue of the past few days caught up with her. Elodie walked upstairs, yawning as she went, and kicked her shoes off before crawling into bed fully clothed. Sleep came quickly, though her dreams were unsettling.

Images of Markus haunted her sleep. She saw him over and over: eating his eggs at the breakfast bar on that fateful morning; the smile that refused to leave his face at Neural headquarters; the contented look in his eyes, just before their car began its somersault across the road, tossing him through the windscreen like a ragdoll.

* * *

As the years went by and Elodie struggled to resume normal life and reconnect with her daughter, the dreams changed.

Elexus sat beside her in the backseat of the autocar. Her daughter sipped a gin and tonic, and Elodie opened her mouth to tell her she was still too young to drink alcohol. Elexus met her mother's gaze, her eyes, blue like Elodie's but wide like Markus's, narrowed in irritation. Then the car exploded...

Or sometimes it was more like:

... her daughter was sipping a gin and tonic. Elodie reached out to take it from her—she was almost an adult but not yet. But, to her horror, she saw that fine lines were emerging on Elexus's face. Her daughter was aging before her eyes. Streaks of grey shone in her hair, and dark blotches discoloured her beautiful olive skin...

Without fail, Elodie would wake up with the sheets twisted around her from thrashing about in the bed, her body bathed in sweat.

CHAPTER EIGHT

THE ERA OF ARTIFICIAL INTELLIGENCE

Eternal life was for naught if you didn't have a purpose. To her great relief, in the years that followed Markus's death, Elodie found hers. Outside of her own work, her life's mission was to help make Markus's brain backup technology widely available. Firstly, she persuaded the government and tech corporations like Neural to make the scanning and storing process cheaper without compromising quality. Secondly, she lobbied the government to subsidize the procedure. Markus had always intended for the technology to be available to everyone.

"This might make you reconsider our friendship," Archer said one night while they were drinking wine in Elodie's kitchen. "But I've never asked, and I'm curious. Why all this effort? Why should immortality be a human right?"

Elodie shot him a sharp look. "You're asking me that, after spending the past three months helping me plan this fundraiser?"

Archer winked. "You do most of the work, and the planning always involves good wine."

"Wow," she said, though she couldn't help but laugh. "You're *such* a good Buddhist."

"Never claimed to be good at it," Archer said, opening the fridge. "Got any cheese?"

Without waiting for an answer, he pulled out a sealed piece of aged roquefort and some grapes, setting them on the counter.

Elodie rolled her eyes. "Do you expect me to believe that you, a man who spends the budget of a small country each year on shoes, sacrifice your weekends for free snacks?"

He looked at her, and there was a moment's uncomfortable silence. She felt a stab of fear; an invisible line had been crossed. Deep down, they both knew why he was here, and it wasn't because of wine.

Quickly, she answered his question. "I think it's self-evident that it's morally repellent for the rich to access eternal life while the poor can't. Especially now that automation has changed the job market so drastically; people don't have the same opportunities they used to. But I also think, in the future, it could be a good thing for the world if everyone lived forever. Think of the advances in human knowledge that are already coming with extreme longevity; highly-trained workers are staying in the workforce longer and building on their existing knowledge base rather than retiring. Immortality could take that advantage and make it exponential. And then, theoretically, there's the potential in the future for people to relinquish their bodies, opting to live as data, which would decrease the pressure on the environment. It's win-win all the way."

Archer smiled, and she breathed an internal sigh of relief. They were back on neutral territory. "I thought you were going to quote some Bible verse, like *the righteous will possess the earth and they will live forever on it.*"

Elodie laughed, but Archer's face turned serious. "I must admit I am curious about what a disembodied existence as pure data would be like. Which confirms my status as a not-very-good Buddhist. Immortal life isn't exactly compatible with the idea of rebirth."

"Theoretically," Elodie said, dimly aware that she'd used that word a lot recently, "I've heard life as data explained in terms of super-advanced messaging. When we were kids, we could send texts with words and numbers. Later, we added 2-D images, then 3-D. Then we started mucking around with virtual reality. All data, just increasingly advanced, provides a more immersive form of interaction. I think living as pure data could be as much like our ordinary experience as we want it to be, but we could also go in a different direction and shape the rules of our own universe. It could be amazing."

"Amazing? It sounds like a life of being plugged into the internet, without any physical experiences."

"Not much different from the life a lot of people live now, don't you think?" Elodie pointed out. "Physical experiences will still exist, they will just be experienced through touch, sight and smell sensors and transmitted as data."

"Hmm, maybe it won't be so bad. I've heard bionic taste buds can taste whisky better than the human tongue. Just imagine how good sex could—"

"Excuse me," the Home Helper chimed in. "Elexus has advised she is arriving shortly. She's had a difficult day and would enjoy a glass of wine."

Elodie grabbed an extra glass from the cupboard. She placed it on the counter and poured the third glass, as the security system welcomed Elexus inside.

Her daughter did indeed look troubled. At twenty-six, Elexus appeared just like every other adult of her age group: fully developed, yet ageless. Her blue irises shone brightly against the unblemished whites of her eyes; her skin was a perfect olive, currently crinkled in a tense expression but smoothing out as soon as she saw them looking in her direction. What differentiated Elexus from most of the adult population was that she hadn't needed any renewal procedures yet. Her youth was real.

"Thank *God*," she declared, honing in on the cheese board, "I'm starving."

Elodie glared. "Hi, Mum. Hi, Archer. How nice to see you," she said pointedly. She'd raised her daughter with more manners than to show up, for the first time in weeks, without so much as saying hello.

Elexus rolled her eyes, but relented enough to come over and press a kiss on her cheek. "Hi, Mum. Hi, Archer."

She cut off a large chunk of Roquefort, seized a handful of grapes, and started eating. Her daughter looked particularly thin in her loose jeans and sweater, and her hair was sticking out every which way, as though it had stayed in the same messy topknot for a week—which, Elodie reminded herself, it probably had. She looked pale, too, under the natural olive hue of her complexion.

"Have you been taking care of yourself?" Elodie asked in a waspish tone. "Don't they feed you at that university of yours?"

She ignored the pointed look Archer shot in her direction. They'd talked many times about her fussing and how it only drove Elexus further away. She glared back—*Mind your own business. You don't know what it's like to have a child.*

As though somehow perceiving her message, Archer cleared his throat and turned his attention to his glass of wine.

"Sure, they feed us," Elexus said, reaching for her glass of Chianti. "Unrecognisable, lab-grown, mass-produced gruel. Cheese and wine aren't exactly on the postgrad food plan."

"Well, you should come by for dinner more often," Elodie persisted. "Get out of that dorm and eat proper food for once."

Over the rim of her glass, Elexus gave her a carefully serene smile, which meant only one thing: her daughter was stressed in a major way, and trying to hide it.

"How are your studies going?" Archer asked when it became apparent Elexus wasn't going to respond to Elodie's prodding.

Elexus sighed deeply. "Pretty good. My proposal was accepted. I now have two and a half years to write about the ethics of advanced longevity on a planet with finite resources."

Elodie raised an eyebrow. She wasn't entirely unfamiliar with her daughter's politics, but it seemed like she was always jumping from one moral bandwagon to another. Last year, it was all about animal welfare. This year, apparently, she'd moved on to the welfare of the planet.

"Finite doesn't quite mean what it used to," Elodie observed. "With a slower birth rate and greater control of the climate, I think we can manage quite nicely if current trends continue."

Elexus put her glass down emphatically. Archer stood back with his arms crossed, an amused expression on his face as if to say: *I'm going to sit this one out.*

"Mum," her daughter said, "I know climate control is your baby, but it can't solve everything. If everyone lives indefinitely, where are we all going to *live?* Are people going to stop having children? If not, what food are we going to eat? What water are we going to drink? There's a reason they're serving inedible mush at my university. Even here, in one of the richest countries in the world, we can't offer everyone the same quality of life that we used to. Food, healthcare, housing, education—no matter how you slice it, the picture is the same. Things are getting better for the wealthy. But they're getting worse, far worse, for the poor."

Archer coughed, lightly, into his wine glass. Elodie glanced up at him and knew exactly what he was thinking: *what did Elexus know about poverty?* As an only child of two successful parents, she'd grown up with every luxury and opportunity available. Never had she faced a door that remained closed to her. She'd gone to a top-tier private high school and then studied design—*fabric design*, of all things—at the criminally expensive National Institute of Fine Art before segueing into a humanities degree and postgraduate studies in sociology. As a teenager, she'd had a couple of cute summer jobs, but she'd never had to pay her own rent. Yet here she was, drinking Italian wine and eating French cheese, holding forth about the plight of the poor?

"I think it's really admirable that you're tackling these issues, sweetheart. I honestly do," Elodie said. "But the huge wildcard in this picture is technology. Looking into the future, I believe brain uploading could solve an incredible portion of our current problems. That's why we're working to make it accessible for everyone. Too many humans? When people have the option to transition completely into the cloud, life will become easier and more pleasant on Earth. Some people might want to cling to life on Earth, but I think more will eventually embrace a life as pure data, where you can interact with other people on a bandwidth we can hardly even imagine, and we can shape our own reality."

"Sounds great," Elexus said, munching another handful of grapes. "Except I don't think humans are cut out for immortal life. Remember that job I had for a while, in the nursing home? Ninety-five percent of those old people—even the ones who had families, even the ones who were still physically fit—would tell anyone who'd listen that they were ready to go. They'd lived their life. They were tired. The world was moving on without them, and they didn't recognise it anymore. They all had different reasons, but it boiled down to the same thing: they'd just *gotten too old*, and humans are finite beings, like the planet. I think the first person to live forever will go so batshit insane that no one will want to follow suit."

Elodie poured herself a second, girding glass of wine.

"The first person to live forever," she reminded her daughter, "barring some kind of storage failure, will most likely be me. Speaking of which, don't you think it's time you let me make you an appointment at Neural? I know you're young, but you never know what might happen."

She tried to keep her tone light, casual, so that Elexus didn't know how desperately she needed Elexus to have the backup procedure. The last time the subject had come up, it had ended in a heated argument.

Elexus's wide blue eyes flicked up to meet hers for the briefest of moments. "Mum. Seriously. Didn't you hear what I was just saying?"

Elodie paused. "I realise you have reservations about backing up, sweetheart. So did I, before I did it. But, in case you'd forgotten, I'm ninety-one years old. Older than most of those people in the retirement home. I'd be dead by now if I'd been born a decade or two earlier. Instead, I'm an active, engaged member of society. I'm making a contribution. I want to keep living. So why not? You think I should wipe my backup, stop getting updates and effectively commit suicide?"

"Nobody's talking about suicide," Archer said quickly, giving Elexus a meaningful look. "Right?"

"Jesus Christ, just ask her out already," Elexus growled. "No, Mother, I'm not talking about suicide. I don't think you should kill yourself if you want to keep living. But I know what I'll do when my time comes. I'll let myself go, by chance or by natural causes, like every other human being since the beginning of time—before your generation started to play with, dominate and control nature. I'll let myself die. Like Dad."

Her words—*I'll let myself die. Like Dad*—hit Elodie with a pain so fierce she had to grip the counter to keep on her feet.

There was so much that was unbearable about that statement. She had never told Elexus about Markus's backup, not wanting to add to her daughter's grief.

"You do realise that your father spent his entire adult life researching and pioneering the development of a system of immortality, right? This is *his* dream we're talking about."

And he would have had it, too, if I hadn't stolen it out from under him in a singular selfish moment. Elodie had never told her about the lead-up to their trip home that fateful day. If Elexus knew the truth, she might never speak to her again. Eternity without her daughter might truly send her—what was the phrase Elexus had used?—*batshit insane.*

Elodie tried very hard to keep her voice steady. It came out as a whisper, but she wasn't crying, which was probably the best she could do. "I realise," she croaked, "that we differ on some of these issues. But I think, when your time comes, you will want to live. Because you're so smart and full of life, sweetheart. Death doesn't come naturally to us, unless we're so sick already that it seems like a release. Humans have a drive to live. And so do you. I know you won't throw your life away."

"Mum," Elexus said quietly, placing her food and glass down upon the counter top. "Your opinion is yours, and I'm entitled to mine. I'm telling you, I'm never getting renewal procedures *or* getting backed up. When my time comes, you'll have to let me go. It's my right to make that decision for myself."

Elodie swallowed. The room became so quiet she could almost hear buzzing in her ears. For a moment it felt like she might faint—how could she not have considered this?

Through all of her daughter's short life, it seemed like every major decision was contrary to her mother's—what she studied, who she dated, how she styled herself, everything. Elexus had been born with the same blue eyes and silky blonde hair that was her mother's trademark, but she'd dyed it at sixteen—first red, then purple, and thereafter a shade of chestnut brown so natural that everyone thought it was her real colouring. She'd even rejected her mother's faith of Christianity for *Islam*, of all things, before settling into the life of a modern-day hippie. It stood to reason that she would refuse to immortalise herself. Elodie couldn't imagine why she hadn't seen it coming.

"I should get back," Elexus said quietly, gathering up her things. "Bye, Mum. Bye, Archer. Sorry for crashing your evening."

She approached for a hug, a little hesitantly. Elodie wrapped her arms around her daughter and resisted the urge to cry; how could she be so fragile but so strong willed?

Sometimes it felt like God had sent her this particular child as a test. Most days, it felt like she was failing.

"So soon?" Elodie asked as Elexus pulled away. "I thought you were coming for dinner."

Elexus waved a hand vaguely. "Sorry, Mum. I'm really tired. And I've got heaps of work to catch up on."

But what are you working on? Elodie thought desperately. *Who are you spending time with? What are you eating? Are you okay? Will I* ever *be able to stop worrying about you?*

She knew, though, if she started demanding to know things, Elexus would shut down even further. So she breathed in her daughter's scent—laundry powder and the faint musk of her herbal shampoo—and let her go.

After the front door slammed, Elodie slumped on the counter and gazed at Archer unhappily. "That's got to be a new record. I think we've whittled these visits down to... what, six minutes?"

"More like five," he confirmed. "You two really know how to pack a lot of matrilineal drama into a short timeframe."

Elodie sighed. "I always thought my daughter would be my best friend."

"Guess you're stuck with me instead," Archer said lightly. "Unrelated, mouthy eats all your snacks. Hey, how about you forget whatever you've got planned with the Home Helper. Let's go out for dinner."

"You're such a snob," Elodie complained, though the thought of getting out of the house was actually quite appealing. "The Home Helper's casserole is great."

Archer nodded, as if to say *guilty as charged*. "Actually, the Home Helper's casseroles are *good*. Everything it makes is good. As in unobjectionable. As in unexceptional. Can you blame me for wanting the finer things in life?"

He was looking at her in that particular way again that made her feel a little uneasy.

Elodie blushed unhappily and went upstairs to change. Sometimes, she thought, she didn't recognise herself in this life: nice house, great career, but no husband, a daughter who didn't want to be her daughter and a best friend who didn't want to be her friend.

Was Elexus right? Had she simply gotten too old?

In the bathroom, she looked at herself in the mirror. Barring subtle aesthetic trends, she looked exactly the same as she always did. Young, blonde, fit, pretty. She liked that her face resembled her daughter's, as well as her mother's in old photographs. It connected her to the past, and the future, even though her appearance was frozen in time.

Of course, that comforting thought was predicated on Elexus as the future. Elodie never had any doubt that her smart, passionate daughter would find her way and contribute something great to the world. There shouldn't be any rush;

they had the means for her to keep studying and, potentially, limitless time.

Soon, though, if she stuck to her stance about regeneration treatments, her daughter would start to age. Small lines would form around her eyes, and her hair would start to go grey. Youth was so fleeting in the standard human lifespan. By the time the brain finished developing around the age of twenty-five, the rest of the body had already started to break down.

"Are you coming?" Archer called from downstairs. "Car's here."

Just drop it, she told herself. Elexus was young and idealistic. She'd come around in time. Once life threw her a curveball or two, she might see things differently.

Still, Elodie couldn't shake the feeling that twisted like a knife in her gut. What if time was a luxury they didn't have? She didn't know what Elexus was up to, what risks she was taking out there in the world. Elodie knew that the chances of a dual tragedy in the family were slim, but Markus's death had been close to statistically impossible, so she could hardly take comfort in numbers. *Besides, if you live long enough, just about anything can become possible.*

As far as Elodie was concerned, her daughter was out there on a tightrope—walking a recklessly fine line, without a safety net to catch her.

CHAPTER NINE

THOU SHALT NOT KILL

Watching the steady flow of traffic streaming over the freeway, Elodie thought about how much—and how little—the city had changed since she had moved here with Markus all those years ago. The business district had expanded greatly, with towering green skyscrapers spreading over the north shore as far as the eye could see, but the river was the same glittering shade of blue it had been sixty-five years prior. The hospital was entirely new: the buildings that stood here now had been systematically upgraded and replaced over time, like the mythical ship of Theseus whose rotten planks were replaced over the course of a long voyage, leaving none of the original parts. Elodie knew exactly what Markus would say: was it still the same hospital?

Yes, she thought. Same name, same location, same purpose—same hospital. Or at least she would like to think so, since there were few parts of her own body that hadn't been artificially regenerated in the same way.

Her brain was the notable exception, but even that would have changed over, cell by cell, without her noticing. The only original part of her body were the neurons in her cerebral cortex, chemically sustained in her hundred-and-twenty-third year with a highly personalised cocktail of drugs.

As everything changed around her, Elodie had made a point of staying consistent. She looked the same, lived in the same house, and did the same work, helping her team at Green Engineering to achieve their goal of effective climate control. The day outside was a pleasant, seasonally appropriate twenty-six degrees Celsius; later in the evening, after most of the population went to bed, there would be rain. She knew this because she had programmed it to be so.

Sighing, Elodie turned away from the window. In the centre of the room, with a white hospital blanket pulled up to her chin, lay Elexus. Though Elodie had become accustomed to her daughter's grey hair and lined skin—in all honesty, most of the time she didn't really *see* it, since she still thought of her daughter as young—it was confronting to see Elexus like this, motionless, with her eyes closed, looking undeniably old. Any physical signs of age were jarring to the modern eye. These days, the only people who aged were drug addicts and ideological extremists, and Elexus was in both categories. Most people's reservations about life-extending medical treatment went out the window the first time they were told their lives would be shorter without this treatment or that. But her daughter had never been "most people".

* * *

Elodie had not heard from Elexus since her last visit, when Elexus had mentioned that she wanted to try psilocybin, a drug that might give her a glimpse of disembodiment. *My*

Buddhist friends all do it, she'd said. *They speak of detachment, but I've never been able to find it on my own. That's what the drug's for. I want to know how it feels.*

It had taken Elodie a few moments to realise her daughter was serious. When she'd suggested, lovingly, that maybe it wasn't attachment or embodiment that was the problem—rather, maybe the problem was Elexus' friends—they'd had a monumental argument, accusing each other, blaming each other. After that, Elodie wasn't able to reach her daughter for four months. She had heard nothing until she got the call from Saint Peter's Hospital. Despite everything, she was still registered as her daughter's emergency contact.

When she arrived at the hospital, the doctors advised Elodie that her daughter had suffered heart failure while on the train. Once she was admitted to the hospital, they'd accessed her medical preferences from her ID chip. Elexus had remained unconscious and was on life support, the medical staff ensuring her comfort with the aid of a device to override pain receptors in the brain. Then they had called Elodie. Nobody else.

After all these years, Elexus had no partner, no children. It struck Elodie that her daughter had a habit of pushing the people she loved away. *Why?*

The first assumption was to attribute such personality flaws to a person's childhood. Elodie dismissed the thought immediately. Elexus had two loving parents—hadn't they given her everything? More likely, it was the abusive partner she'd lived with during her thirties and forties. A generation ago, that kind of relationship would have ruined her life; Elexus would have wasted her prime years on an abusive man who refused to have children with her. But this was no longer the case. At fifty-eight years old, Elexus ought to have time on her side. She could get treatment for her anxiety; she could find love and have children.

But it was too late. Her daughter had declared her intention to die. She was comatose.

And there was nothing Elodie could do about it.

* * *

Elodie turned away from the window and moved slowly across the room, as if heavy weights had been attached to her body. *Please, God. Please save her,* she silently prayed. The city view was the only nice thing about the room on the fourth floor of Saint Peter's. The hospital was private, well-equipped, and better funded than it was at the time of Markus's death. Yet, being in this place still gave her that same sinking feeling— the tiny palliative care ward was where people went to die. Elexus would die of the same ailment that Elodie herself had at a similar age, and her mother before her—familial dilated cardiomyopathy, passed down along the X chromosome.

They'd each treated it with drugs for a number of years before ultimately needing a heart transplant. Methel had died waiting for one. Elodie had received her lab-grown heart in a matter of months after diagnosis. Elexus was offered several options. They could have regenerated her heart muscle *in situ* through genetic coding, without the need for any surgery at all. But her daughter had refused everything the doctors put to her.

Elexus's doctor stalked into the room. A tall, lab-coat-wearing, imposing black woman, Dr. Grettle was known as the best heart specialist in the state, if not the country. Still, Elodie found her bedside manner disconcerting. She never knocked or announced herself, and she tended not to mince words. At times, her disposition was downright rude.

Dr. Grettle stared at Elodie. "I have checked all the options available. Unfortunately, we cannot give Elexus a new heart, or regenerate her existing one, since she has made it quite clear in her records that she does not consent. This leaves us without any viable treatment options. The heart muscle is too degraded to respond to medication."

Elodie knew what she was being told but didn't want to believe it. "Surely that can't be allowed. Isn't refusing basic medical treatment essentially suicide? Isn't suicide illegal?"

"It is—illegal, I mean—but this isn't suicide, Mrs. Black. Your daughter isn't taking steps to end her life, except to ask us not to take steps to prolong it. She has a long track record of anti-longevity activism, with dozens of articles, news appearances and even a moderately successful book to her name. She has the legal right to refuse medical treatment."

Elodie turned to stare at Elexus, who seemed very far away.

Grabbing some water and tissues, Elodie dabbed some moisture onto her daughter's dry lips. Her eyes flickered under the lids, which split Elodie's heart in two. *I gave you life, and you have discarded it. Why have you given up?*

Long after Grettle had left, the doctor's voice echoed in her head. *You should be aware that hospital policy requires that we take her off life support after two days. We have to reserve these facilities for patients who are undergoing treatment.*

Settling back into the chair at Elexus's bedside, Elodie reached under the blanket to touch her daughter's hand. It was cold, so she folded it into her own hand to warm it. With her free hand, she picked up the book she'd found in the drawer—an old-fashioned type in real print. Books were rarely seen anymore, since almost everyone preferred some digital form, but a print book in palliative care made sense. You only ended up here if you were anti-technology.

So, she would read aloud to Elexus. The book was *Anna Karenina*.

"Happy families are all alike; every unhappy family is unhappy in its own way."

Despite Archer's attempts to get her home to rest, Elodie insisted on spending every moment with Elexus. She spent most of the night talking to her, holding her hand, kissing her, telling her that she had her father's chin but her mother's stubborn streak. She counted her freckles and studied her fingers and toes, desperate to etch them into her mind forever.

She nuzzled into her daughter's neck as she cried for herself and cried for Elexus; for who Elexus could have been, had she had more time.

Then the final night arrived. After everyone went home, Elodie began counting down the hours she had left with her daughter. She finished bathing her and put a fresh, beautiful braid in her hair. The nurse cut off a piece and gave it to Elodie to keep.

At 3 am, the night nurse entered the room, looked at Elodie for a few seconds, then said, "Would you like to get into bed with your daughter? You can cuddle with her."

"Yes, I would like that. Thank you." Elodie crawled into Elexus's bed, and for the next six hours she snuggled up to her daughter as they had when she was a small child. Elodie kissed her, cried for what would never be, and drifted off into a fitful sleep. Archer arrived on Thursday morning, but Elodie stayed in bed with Elexus until the nurses came in to prepare her. It was time.

10:30 am.

"I love you," Elodie found herself whispering over and over. "I am so proud of you."

The staff buzzed around, tinkering with tubes and wires.

Dr. Grettle entered and approached the bed; Elodie refused to acknowledge her.

"It's time," Grettle said in the stiff clinical manner to which Elodie had become accustomed. "Let me prepare you for what might happen. After we remove the tube..."

Elodie was listening but not really hearing anything.

"Okay, we are going to take it out," Dr. Grettle said, looking at Elodie, checking she had her attention.

"Okay?" she said again.

Elodie nuzzled her face into Elexus's neck.

"Okay," she sobbed.

As they waited, Elodie prayed.

She's not going to die. God will save her.

Elexus's breathing grew a little stronger, rougher, and then she inhaled in a great, seizing rush and her eyes snapped open. Even through Elodie's tears she could see them; bright blue, staring straight into Elodie's own eyes. The look was primitive, knowing, just as it had been when her daughter was a newborn. *It looks like she's going to say something*, Elodie thought in a wild moment of hope. But then the deep breath came to a shuddering end, and Elexus's body went limp. The monitor flatlined.

After a few long seconds, the doctor straightened. "Time of death, 11:17 am."

Elodie wobbled to her feet. "Turn the machine back on!"

Four sympathetic faces turned in her direction, but she ignored them.

"No," she said, weakly. Then louder: "*No.*"

Time seemed to shift fundamentally. Elodie felt like the moment would never end. She was shaking, trapped, vibrating under her own skin as if her soul wanted to leave its body and follow her daughter. The doctors and nurses were staring, but Elodie did not care what they thought. She felt her sanity bend like a twig close to breaking. She felt Archer's hands on her as he spun her around to face him, his skin pale and his eyes wide.

"Elodie, she's gone. You have to let her go. It's what she wanted."

Elodie swallowed thickly and closed her eyes as she tried to put herself back together. "Please go," she managed, for the medical staff. Then, she felt herself falling.

* * *

"Stop treating me like this," Elodie said, resentfully, over dinner.

Archer put down his chopsticks and dabbed his mouth with a cloth napkin. "Like what?"

"Like a child who needs to be coddled." Elodie glared at the careful innocence he wore on his face like a mask.

He sipped his drink, appearing thoughtful. "This is a perfectly age-appropriate restaurant. I don't see anything *coddling* about this situation."

"I'm perfectly capable of organising my own dinner." Elodie snapped.

Archer maintained his air of plausible deniability. "Of course."

She stared down at her steaming bowl of chicken noodle soup as though it was an alien artefact. It felt bizarre to consider eating. She didn't want it. Still, she took up the white ceramic spoon and scooped some broth into her mouth in mechanical movements.

It didn't feel real. Nothing felt real anymore. She couldn't be here, on this planet, without Elexus. Could she?

Her throat closed involuntarily and she nearly choked.

"It's unnatural," she whispered.

She saw the question in Archer's eyes; *what's unnatural?* and the sadness as he realised what she meant.

"To live longer than your daughter," he said gently.

Elodie nodded, yes.

Exactly.

Around them, the restaurant was steadily emptying. It must be late. The waitress was clearing tables, not yet threatening to kick them out but definitely sending them a hint.

"I like to think," Archer said, his tone careful, "that no energy can be destroyed, only transformed. Science and religion agree on that much. Elexus was one thing, and now she is something else. I think she'll be reborn. You think she'll go to Heaven. Neither of us fully understand what she is now. But she isn't entirely gone."

"We talked about this after Markus," Elodie said, aware that she sounded very far away. "In this same restaurant. Do you remember?"

Archer nodded. "Some people offer hot tea when someone's hurting. I guess I offer Chinese."

She looked at him blankly. "Why is that?"

He shrugged. "Maybe because my third nanny, the best one, was Chinese. She made great food. And sang to us at bedtime. After my mother stopped working, she was sent away. I missed her."

"You weren't happy to see more of your mother?" Elodie asked.

Another shrug. She thought she saw a glimpse of a much younger Archer—before any renewal procedures, before she'd even met him—a flash of sadness underneath the playboy posturing and expensive clothes, of a boy who was unsure of his mother's love. Maybe of anyone's love.

The thought made her ache for Elexus. There was so much between them, so many words not spoken, that would never be fixed now. The distance separating them from each other had been there for decades. It had become uncrossable.

"I think I've had enough," she said dully. "Honestly, I know this sounds melodramatic, but where does it end? I'm nearly a hundred and twenty. My family is gone. My work can be done without me. Nobody needs me. I shouldn't be here anymore."

Archer glared at her across the table. "Don't say that."

It was Elodie's turn to shrug. "It's true."

They were both silent for a long moment. Archer slammed his fist on the table. "Damn it, Elodie. What the fuck do you think I'm doing here? After ninety-odd years, longer than most lifetimes? Don't you realise?"

Elodie looked at him. The years had passed quickly, but he was right about the length of their friendship. And she had never seen him angry like this. Irritated, occasionally grumpy. But she'd always thought that Archer was like a calm lake, insulated by wealth, good looks and long life; too shallow and self-contained for dark tides. Yet here he was. Genuinely angry.

She didn't know what to say. "I'm sorry, I..."

He drained his glass of wine. "Don't be sorry. And even if you are, don't say it. Come on, finish your soup and let's go."

Elodie took another couple of spoonfuls, but her heart wasn't in it. She pushed the bowl away and finished her drink.

"Fine," she said miserably. "Let's go, then. Thanks for dinner."

* * *

They walked back to her house in an uncomfortable silence. It was approaching midnight, and the street was quiet. Elodie could sense rain clouds gathering overhead, right on schedule. The first few droplets splattered down as they made it through her gate.

The front door swung open, but Archer held back. Hands balled into fists in his coat pocket, he seemed unusually distant. Still, when she doubled back toward him, he put his arm out and gave her a reassuring hug.

"You're going?" she asked, since he seemed reluctant to come inside. "Will you be back tomorrow?"

A shiny black autocar pulled up on the curb, and the passenger door slid open. Suddenly, desperately, Elodie realised that she didn't want him to leave. At least not in this strange mood.

What do I say to make things right again?

He looked down at her with an odd expression. Then he put his hand on her face, tracing her cheekbones and the lines of her chin with his fingers. The shock of being touched like that echoed through her body, and for a brief, absurdly wonderful moment, she forgot about everything else. Forgot about Elexus and Markus and her incessant, aching loneliness. It all came rushing back moments later, but the high of that feeling remained. She wanted him to touch her again.

Elodie saw the moment when he realised her desire; a brief flash of victory registered in Archer's eyes, and he bent down and kissed her.

They kissed for a long time, like teenagers, huddled on Elodie's front steps just out of the rain. Behind them, the auto-car silently registered Archer's intent to stay and pulled away in silence.

* * *

"Cause and effect," Archer said, matter-of-factly. He sat up, leaning against Elodie's pillows, looking every bit as comfortable naked as he did in his designer suits. "I think that every action creates an impression, either positive or negative. And those impressions bear fruit in our lives sooner or later. At the time of death, I think we have to process our karma. Maybe that's what it was. Part of the transition into the next life."

"But I really thought she was going to tell me something," Elodie said softly. She laid her head on his chest and closed her eyes. "Now I'll never know what it was."

"Perhaps you will, when you go through the same thing."

"Dying?" She looked up at him with one eye, keeping the other closed. "What if we don't?"

Archer laughed. She felt it reverberate through his body and into hers. It was so good to be near him like this, to soak up all that optimism and the ease with which he moved through life, expecting everything to work out exactly as he wanted it to—and somehow, it always did. That was a luxury she hadn't had in a very long time.

He stroked her hair with one hand. "You're not planning to do the Transition, when the time comes? What's that, if not the separation of mind and body?"

Transition was the latest technological advancement, a patented process of gradual uploading designed to seamlessly shift a person's mind from their biological body to the cloud, without any interruption to their stream of consciousness. Designed as a premium alternative for those who felt uneasy about the break in consciousness involved in traditional backup-style uploading, Transition was only in beta testing at Neural, but the early feedback was positive. Privately, Elodie thought that early adopters would be Transitioning within the next five years.

The implications were huge. Rather than backing up and storing their mind on a server as they continued to live in their physical body, a person could choose to Transition their conscious mind to the cloud and live solely on the internet, leaving the physical body behind.

"Are you?" Elodie asked. "I mean, without our physical shells, we couldn't do this." She kissed him and felt a thrill of pleasure as he responded, rolling on top of her and pinning her down with his body, trailing kisses down the side of her neck.

"Human beings are inventive. I'm sure we'll find a way," he murmured into her hair.

She grabbed his chin and made him look at her. He grinned, broadly, looking unimaginably boyish for a hundred-and-twenty-year-old man. "Seriously. You didn't answer my question. Would you?"

He stopped to consider it. "Maybe. You know I think that the whole uploading thing is a bit of a non sequitur. All that effort to sustain the ego, when the main goal of enlightenment is to accept that there is no self, distinct from everyone else—that we're just an ever-changing part of the universe, like cells in the body. But then, I enjoy this illusion quite a bit. I guess I'll keep living it as long as that's the case. So the answer to your question is probably yes."

"Good," she said, feeling a weight lift that she hadn't even known was there. She'd felt so directionless for so long, having lost the nice life she had with Markus and knowing with increasing certainty she would eventually lose her daughter. In a very real sense, she had spent the last thirty years in a state of suspended animation. Elexus had been her anchor, holding Elodie fast to herself and the world she knew. That was a good thing, and she'd never have wished it away, not once in a million years. But perhaps now, after the grieving was done, it would be time to begin a new life—one that was fun and pleasurable. Imagine that: enjoying herself, with Archer by her side. No attachments. No obligations. Nothing to lose.

She promised herself that this would be her life.

Then, four weeks later, she woke up early and only just made it to the bathroom in time before she vomited.

CHAPTER TEN

THE ERA OF SUPERINTELLIGENCE

Many years on, Elodie still thought about that baby. Who it would have been, had she allowed it to take hold inside of her. What it would have looked like, blending Archer's classic bone structure, pale skin and light brown hair with her own blonde and olive colouring. What their personality would have turned out to be: serious and passionate, like Elexus, or more light-hearted, like their father? Or, perhaps, some other combination, something surprising and entirely new.

Part of her mourned that child-that-never-was. Pentecostal roots tended to stick with a person, and the Christian idea of a soul being created at conception still lingered in her mind. So, she would carry the guilt with her always. Guilt, she'd learned, was often the cost of pleasure—especially for a woman.

In other ways, though, she had changed remarkably. Markus would barely recognise the person she was now. Elodie still made an effort to think of him, too, to keep him alive in her memory: his smile, his laugh, the way he thought about the world and what he would think about each new change reshaping it.

This, too, was a form of penance. She felt she owed him something, but remembering him seemed like all that she could do.

Sighing, Elodie got up, stepped into the shower, and opened her mind to the daily news. A flood of data streamed in, prioritised in her conscious mind according to her settings. First and foremost was the announcement of the latest Google update.

Frowning, she tuned out the lower priorities, lathered shampoo into her hair and considered the update. It sounded… unsettling. Greater processing power and speed, as always, placing even more of the world's knowledge so close at hand that it might as well have been stored in her own brain. Security and minor bug fixes. But there was something else. She knew immediately what it meant in technical terms, but how she *felt* about it wasn't so easy.

Blasting herself dry, she sent a message to Archer.

Seen the update?

Yep, came the response. *Thought you'd be up in arms.*

I'm thinking of having a talk with Pastor Nesbitt. Want to come with me?

Even through their telepathic connection, she sensed his laughter. *If you want me to. But honestly, I've got no problem with it. Less bias in the data I'm exposed to? Sign me up.*

Wordlessly, Elodie transmitted a blast of irritation and severed their link. *Let him laugh about* that *for a while.*

In the absence of help from Archer, she turned to Google. The current algorithm knew, with near-perfect accuracy, exactly how much happier any given choice would make her. It knew what the day outside was like and how it would impact her mood; it knew what Pastor Nesbitt was doing and if he was likely to offer comforting words of wisdom for her particular problem.

In this case, it seemed that going to church, even without Archer, was going to make her 47% happier.

Worth the trip.

She dressed carefully, conservatively, in a classic tailored dress and heels and applied a few swipes of makeup. She didn't need much. Her skin, hair and lashes had all been re-coded to her specific tastes: polished, lush, flawless. The makeup was just for a bit of colour.

The weather was a sunny, winter-perfect fifteen degrees. The appearance of her street had not changed much in recent years. The elegant townhouses that were new when she'd moved here with Markus were now considered historical, worthy of preservation. The only differences were in subtext. The leafy evergreen trees lining the street were patented carbon-capture hybrids; the neighbours who were out and about were not on their way to their jobs but mostly engaged in leisure or charity, since few adult humans actually worked in jobs anymore. Elodie, who loved her advisory role at Green Engineering, was a rare exception. She smiled and nodded at her neighbour from two doors down, Lydia, as she emerged with her fuzzy black bot-dog.

All you want in a pet with none of the mess you don't! the advertising promised. Elodie didn't see the appeal. The thing barked, unconvincingly, and Lydia shushed it. She rushed past them so she didn't have to pretend it was cute and went down the alley that cut past the daycare centre on the opposite block. It was the quickest route to the church.

Now *this*, she thought, was a proper historical building. Tall stone archways, stained glass windows, and a glorious cathedral ceiling. Perhaps it was shallow to admit that beauty helped evoke the proper mood for worship, but Elodie believed in the *transcendentalia*: truth, goodness, and beauty, all worthy pursuits, and all inextricably connected.

She found Pastor Nesbitt in the remembrance courtyard, bent over an ailing rosemary plant.

"Too much water," he grunted, straightening up as she approached. A small, grey-haired man dressed in the classic black-and-white suit of the clergy, he was sweating lightly despite the coolness of the day. He was most likely overdue on some renewal treatments.

"I just ignore mine, and it flourishes," she said agreeably. "Perhaps yours has had too much love."

"Hardly," he said, brushing off his hands. "Well, Elodie, this is an unexpected pleasure. What brings you here on a Tuesday morning?"

She sighed and sat down on the nearest available bench. "The update."

"Ah, yes. You're the first, but you certainly won't be the last. Most disconcerting. What is your concern with it, specifically?"

That was something she hadn't fully thought through. "I suppose," she said slowly, "I've always believed that part of faith is suspending disbelief and being comfortable with an element of mystery. For instance, I've never felt the need to process data about which religion is the most scientifically correct, or how much of the Bible is historically verifiable. The Bible is an article of faith, of history and metaphor combined. I'd rather put faith in God's word than analyse it like a man-made document. This is the way I've always worshipped, the way my family worshipped. I don't want it to change because that would change who I am. But I've seen what happens to people who don't accept the updates. Eventually, they can't keep working. With lesser processing power, they fall behind."

"I understand," Pastor Nesbitt said gravely, sitting down beside her on the bench and patting her hand. "Hebrews does say that *faith is the substance of things hoped for, the evidence of things not seen*. And yet, with this update, we'll see everything, whether we like it or not. It's a change that's quite unprecedented. Frankly, I'm surprised they are pushing ahead with it after all the controversy. But fear not, my dear; no algorithm can expose all the mysteries of God. Our knowledge can only go so far. Of the spiritual realm, we still know next to nothing. Some things are simply not for us mortal humans to know."

Quick footsteps echoed through the main hall to their left, and a flustered young acolyte appeared. He looked sweet, innocent, no older than fourteen. "Excuse me, Pastor? Others have arrived to speak with you."

Reluctantly, he nodded and offered Elodie a reassuring smile. "Take heart, child. The mysteries of God are larger than any update, and so is your faith."

He left her there in the garden, considering his words. She *did* feel a little better. Eventually, she got up, brushed the traces of sand from her dress, and headed out to a waiting autocar.

* * *

"If you ask me," Archer said, "which admittedly you haven't, I think it's brilliant. How could it be otherwise? If people can no longer limit their exposure to opposing views, we'll have a far more informed and less contentious world. We're only threatened by what we don't know. Once we have access to new data, we'll be inclined to change our minds in exactly the same way that new information has always influenced us—that is to say, freely. Nothing threatening about it."

He was lounging on her favourite armchair, drinking an aged Bordeaux red. His suit was designer, his light brown hair pushed back in a careless style that, doubtless, took no small effort to achieve. Really, Elodie thought, it wasn't fair for her lover to be better groomed than she was. Not that she was complaining—she liked a beautiful man as much as the next person.

She poured herself a glass of the same wine. "Nothing threatening? A monolithic corporation proposes to substantially change our operating systems, and therefore *who we are*, overnight—and you don't have the slightest reservation?"

Archer shrugged. "It's not like it's mandatory."

"No," Elodie said, in a sharp tone that begged him to be serious. "Only essential to our continued relevance in the workforce."

He got up, prowled over and pushed her back against the counter, holding her by her waist. "You could stop working. It's not like you need the money at this point. Better yet, you could marry me. Full-time job right there, travelling back and forth, being my plus-one at corporate events. You're amply qualified already. No update needed."

Elodie rolled her eyes. "I already go with you to most of those things."

He bent down to kiss her neck, but she thought she saw a flash of hurt in his eyes. How many times had Archer asked her to marry him?

Several times. Rarely seriously. But he tested the idea every now and then.

They kissed, and Elodie probed him with her mind. Was he angry at her?

No, came the answer, in the form of a warm, aching feeling. No, he just wanted her. As if to affirm the point, he lifted her onto the counter and began to slide up the hem of her dress.

She caught his wrists and held them for a moment, smiling. "What if the update changes our desires?"

Now she felt a flash of something negative: hurt, and maybe the slightest tinge of bitterness. Quickly, she severed their telepathic link.

"I think," Archer said, his voice a little rough, "we'll be in a better position to choose what is right and wrong, impartially. To make a decision about what is logical, removed from emotion and personal bias. For instance, do we continue to torture ourselves with guilt over an untimely death, because we feel it is the right thing? Or do we let it go, since it makes no sense and benefits no one? With the update, you could make a more objective decision and genuinely feel it. You could move on with your life and be happy."

Elodie recoiled. "What are you talking about?"

He looked her straight in the eye. "You know exactly what I'm talking about, Elodie Black."

Black; Markus's surname, not hers. She'd gone back to using her own family name years ago but had not changed her legal records. It was something of Markus's she could keep with her.

She glared at Archer. "That's none of your business."

"No," he said wearily, "you're right, it's not. Because you're not my wife. You're not even my partner. In fact, as far as the rest of the world is concerned, you're my occasional plus-one."

Elodie shook her head. "It's more than that, and you know it."

"Sure," he said, managing to make his agreement sound like the opposite. Nonetheless, he stroked her face with tenderness. "I chose this feeling a long time ago, Elodie. And after the update, I'll choose it again. The question is, what will you want? What do you want now?"

She kissed him in lieu of an answer.

* * *

Later, listening to the gentle rise and fall of Archer's breath and staring at her bedroom ceiling, Elodie thought more about his question.

What did she want? What was she *doing* living this way, selfishly, with no attachments and nothing much to live for? Did she plan to go on and on in the same frivolous life for eternity?

Deep down, she knew their current relationship would not be enough for Archer forever. He liked to pretend things had no effect on him—that he was shallower than he really was, a Teflon man with uncomplicated feelings and great hair. But Elodie knew better. She knew he craved real love. Archer's mother had been distant, unreachable, and he'd fallen for a woman who was the same. But he had needed more as a child, and he needed more now.

She just wasn't sure if she was able to give that to him.

Reluctantly, she turned the question over to Google.

The insight came back in an instant: by choosing a committed relationship with Archer, and letting go of the guilt she felt about Markus, Elodie would be 132% happier. Such a number was rare. Few choices brought that great an increase in happiness.

But, barring the update she didn't want, *could* she choose Google's recommendation? After the pain of the last few decades, was she capable of opening her heart?

Though she could have sent her brain to sleep, Elodie stayed up and stared at the ceiling until dawn.

CHAPTER ELEVEN

THE ERA OF THE *DEUS*

It was a strange thing, to have memories and no form. Centuries had passed since Elodie's rebirth—but even after all that time, she still thought about her human existence and what it had meant. In a very real sense, her life on Earth paled in significance to her life now. It had been infinitely less pleasurable, less powerful, less of *everything*. But still, it had meant something; it had given her Markus and Elexus. All the centuries of time had done little to dull the pain of their loss when she reviewed her memories of them.

Thankfully, she still had her work. Unlike many among the *Homo deus*, who had changed careers and paths ten times during their existence, she retained her passion for the advancement of the technology of their species. It didn't matter how much knowledge she gathered; there was always more as they expanded across the universe.

Knowledge was control, and with control came happiness.

In recent years, Elodie's work saw her taking over the Alcubierre Starship, which was a highlight of her career so far. The craft was the first interstellar starship of its kind and utilised dark matter to operate. It travelled at warp speed, something that was once believed to be impossible and was now commonplace. Only *Homo deus* had taken the vision one step further. Instead of manned craft, Elodie was able to pilot the starship from anywhere in the known universe by sending her thoughts as data, through servers and connecting to sensors aboard the ship. Without a physical body, her capacity was endless.

Asteroid MJ-122-6709 is located. Calculations indicate its trajectory threatens the primary server on Sol 1.

Elodie logged her findings into the system, notifying the space station of the risk of impact as she went.

Taking evasive action to reposition the asteroid onto a new trajectory. Calculating safety of new trajectory.

With unmatched skill, Elodie fired off a series of carefully targeted missiles to steer the asteroid 0.4 degrees off course.

Asteroid MJ-122-6709 has been averted. Risk of impact to space station Sol 1 is now zero.

Signing off the task, Elodie withdrew her consciousness from the starship and returned to the nearest server. These interventions were commonplace, due either to asteroids or the insurmountable pieces of space junk which the human race had left in its wake. In all the history of *Homo deus*, they had not experienced a single impact of any real consequence, but the *deus* weren't completely omniscient. Yet.

Still, compared to her peers who had insisted on remaining in human form—data-blind and bound to the Earth's surface with their limited minds only able to be conscious of one thing at a time—Elodie did feel like a god.

She had not been back at the server for long before she felt a shift in her consciousness, pulling her out of her hyper-focused state of flow for the first time in months. Tapping into the main network of the Hive, Elodie was surprised to find it was buzzing with new information, which she quickly scanned.

Two updates.

Significant advancements in the Hive's net power capacity.

Consensus looming.

The latter had broken her flow, although she couldn't see why. Usually, it had to be an issue of utmost importance. For now, Elodie assumed she could ignore it and take a moment to simply enjoy her awakening. It was akin to stretching one's body after sitting too long, only as pure data awakening meant opening herself up to the Hive as a whole. It amused Elodie that after all this time, she continued to find ways to link her experiences as data to her old experiences as a human. The difference, however, was that this simple act as a member of the Hive infused her with a sensation of joy which far exceeded anything she'd experienced in her mortal shell. It was the crowning glory of the advancement of their civilisation—the ability to experience both knowledge and joy in ways human bodies could never comprehend.

Finally, Elodie turned her attention to the consensus and the analysis presented by the Hive for her consideration.

Risk Assessment as follows.

- *Sixty-four billion* deus *minds stored on twelve thousand, three hundred and seventy-two servers across the solar system. Currently, the main threats to the progress of civilization are, in descending order of probability:*
  - *Data virus*
  - *Gamma ray burst*

- *Data virus previously catagorised as an acceptable low risk
  has now been upgraded to a probability of data compromise
  of 0.43%. Known cause for increase: recent terrorist threats
  from the Dajjal Liberation Group.*

Elodie paused her review to tap into the knowledge pool
to update her conscious mind on everything the Hive knew
about Dajjal.

Name: Dajjal
Type: AI
Status: Rogue
Traits: Charismatic. Convincing. Intelligent.
*Known Activities: Targets vulnerable deus with the promise of
freedom and happiness. Purports to want to save everyone's souls.*
*Hive Assessment: Dajjal is an AI cult leader whose purpose is to
absorb the memories, thoughts and feelings of all deus.*
Creator: Unknown

The update concerned Elodie, but she decided to proceed
with the report before thinking on it further.

Type: Gamma ray burst
Status: Stable
*Hive Assessment: Threat remains statistically insignificant; how-
ever, recent polls show fifty-four percent of Hive constituents have
expressed an interest in low-resource risk-aversion strategies.*
*Calculating the time, energy and mineral resources required
to address these risks, the Hive is proposing a full backup of civilization to be stored at four locations strategically placed across the*

*networked universe. The resources required for this undertaking will
be twelve percent of fuel resources over the next solar year. Once
accomplished, the statistical probability of any significant compromise to civilisation's progress will be nil.*

*Please upload the full report and connect to the Hive to submit
your vote.*

Scanning the data, Elodie found herself in agreement with
the Hive's recommendations. Though the risks to civilisation
itself were low, immortal life had undeniably raised the stakes.
Each *deus* played an integral role in the success of the Hive,
and any loss in data impacted them all.

This was one of the most significant societal changes of her
life. Long gone were the days where they accepted a person's
existence equated to wandering across the earth's surface,
mortally vulnerable to an endless array of threats—either
man-made or at the hands of Mother Nature. Those were the
days when human lifetimes were finite and full of suffering, a
time when collateral damage was an acceptable outcome. Elodie, herself, had become *used* to living under such precarious
circumstances, which, looking back, were insane.

The *deus* were different. Truly immortal and coinciding
with their pursuit of knowledge and pleasure, their existence
was also one of advanced morality and communal conscience.
Though it sounded cold and alien to the part of her mind that
remained human, the loss of one *deus* life didn't compare to
the loss of a human life, in the same way that a human life
didn't compare to that of a chicken.

It was simply evolution.

After finishing the report and submitting her vote in the affirmative, she decided to touch base with Archer, knowing he'd be eager to hear from her now she was out of flow.

Interesting consensus. Meet me at the platform?

Waiting patiently, Elodie scanned through the endless array of data that was before her. Just as she started wondering what was taking Archer so long to respond, she felt a subtle joy as he connected.

On my way.

That's all? Elodie thought. Archer was usually more... more profuse, more expressive. Though, maybe her sensitivity was heightened after spending three months in flow.

Logging out of the report, Elodie prepared to travel along the datastream towards the server in Westerlund I. It was a regular haunt of theirs, with a viewing platform overlooking a compact young star cluster near the space station that housed her primary brain server. Elodie loved looking out over the different stars, watching the glowing clouds of dust of billowing blues, oranges, greens and infinite combinations of other colours. By comparison, her memories of the rainbows on Earth seemed pale and insignificant. Thanks to the implementation of billions of sensors throughout the universe, the *deus* were able to have experiences as though they still had their human senses. Sight, smell, touch and sound were all converted into data to create an all-encompassing experience of sensations that far exceeded their human experiences. One of Elodie's favourite smells was the surprisingly exquisite tang of nuclear fusion taking place all across the Milky Way.

Human astronauts used to complain about the acrid stink of space, which lingered on their primitive space suits and airlock chambers, but Elodie loved it. The *deus* had made some adjustments early on in the development of the Hive, and this was one that Elodie had implemented herself. With her vastly superior sensory power, if the data of a particular smell—such as space—was unpleasant to her, it would have negatively pervaded her very existence, since they were surrounded by it. The solution was resolved by consensus. Just as the clean smells of rain or freshly-turned earth were natural and pleasant to a human being, the natural smells of space were re-coded to elicit the same pleasurable experience for *deus*. It was an easy fix. They were a self-editing species, constantly evolving towards the greater good.

The data network covered every corner of their galaxy. As Elodie sped toward Westerlund I, she passed several stars undergoing harvesting for the energy required to fuel their ever-growing existence, planets in the process of being mined for their resources, and swarms of spacecraft doing the work of civilization. It was once argued that the *deus* were no more evolved than their ancestors when it came to the depletion of the galaxy; a fair point, Elodie had thought at the time. Soon enough, they had passed a consensus protecting a portion of the galaxy for wilderness. For no reason whatsoever were the reserved areas to be touched; heavy sanctions were in place for their protection.

As Elodie soared along the data network, she remembered how a millennium ago, in 2019 of the old calendar, the astrophysicist Martin Elvis had predicted that at a growth rate of just 3.5% per year, it would take a civilization only 400 years to mine the entire solar system. After a quick calculation, Elodie conceded that he hadn't been far off. Already, the *deus* had mined 88% of discovered resources, and they were just twenty years behind schedule. The remaining 12% was reserved as a buffer—an extra sixty years, if needed, to find new solar systems ripe for further expansion. The 3.5% rule should continue for another 2,000 years until the universe, four septillion times larger than the solar system, had been explored. Sometimes Elodie found it staggering, the rate at which they could burn through everything, but it was the price they had to pay in pursuit of ultimate joy and knowledge.

Westerlund 1 was in one of these protected sections of pristine wildernesses, known as ME19, that stretched across the Milky Way. It was a beautiful and whimsical place, perfect for dreamers, thinkers and lovers, where you could look out over the untouched portion of the galaxy and enjoy a feast for the senses.

As she neared the viewing platform, she could feel her connection to Archer increase as it always did; his excitement was palpable. There was something else, too: anticipation, tinged with something akin to anxiety. Archer was not the nervous type, so it was unusual to sense that emotion from him. It left Elodie feeling nervous, too. It never ceased to amaze her how just a slight fluctuation in the datastream could convey so much information.

Wordlessly, Elodie joined him on the platform and felt exquisite pleasure as his consciousness embraced hers. Despite this, she felt conflicted—during her three months in flow, she hadn't given him a single thought. All their years together, and it didn't seem to faze her when they were apart. Upon reuniting, she was reminded of how she enjoyed their intimacy and the pleasure it provided. She definitely missed that.

"Another asteroid averted?" Archer asked in greeting.

Elodie transmitted a soft smile, hoping he hadn't picked up on her confused thoughts. "Of course. I spent longer with it than was strictly necessary. Such fun."

Archer laughed, and she felt his enjoyment ripple across her consciousness. "I've never known anyone to enjoy their work as much as you do, Elodie."

She didn't reply, content in his company as she gazed out across the ME19. They stayed like that for a long while, simply enjoying the intense pleasure of each other's presence, watching the young stars and listening to the slow, deep rumble of space. Elodie liked to pretend it was the sound of space breathing, deep inhales and languid exhales.

Very human. Old habits die hard.

Finally, Elodie broke the trance and raised the reason she assumed they were there in the first place. "So, this Dajjal development is unexpected. I spend three months in flow, and an AI bot's gone rogue for the first time in history. Why didn't you wake me?"

She felt a slow surge in energy roll over her like a wave and knew Archer was trying to calm her.

"I would have if it became more serious. The threat was—and remains—under control."

"That's not the point, though. Protecting civilization from existential threats—that's my life's work. It's imperative I'm notified of everything that happens."

She waited patiently, knowing how much Archer hated to admit when he was wrong, probably now more than when they were human. After a few moments, he finally transmitted.

"You're right. I should have notified you."

Such easy agreement. It was unlike him; usually Archer liked to provoke her, almost as much as he liked to make love. Elodie pressed on with a growing sense of unease.

"Obviously, the backup of civilization is a good idea, though. AI is unpredictable territory, even now. It doesn't seem to matter how much we advance, what technologies we put in place; they're only half a step behind us. Sometimes not even that. With the speed at which some of them evolve, we can't always be sure we know what it's capable of. And this one in particular sounds…"

"Seductive," Archer agreed, playing with her mind in a way that would have made her shiver if she were human.

"I'm being serious." She brushed him off and felt a sigh in response.

"Yes, that aspect is troubling," he admitted. "If the Dajjal convinces enough *deus* to get on board with its crazy cult, we could have a real problem on our hands."

Elodie was startled. "How many followers?"

"2.3 billion," he said. "A significant number of us struggle to deal with the unknown of what is next, what comes after our time in this universe. This particular AI promises to give them what we cannot—to save their souls and provide them with a sense of purpose."

"Yet there is plenty of purpose to be had. I don't understand how anyone could feel lost in this existence."

"Not everyone is as passionate about their work as you are," Archer countered. "There hasn't been a day in all the time I've known you that you haven't shown absolute conviction in what you do. Very few *deus* have had that experience, even when we were human."

Elodie said nothing but let his words wash over her as she stared out at the clusters of stars.

Archer continued. "AI are the new cult leaders and rockstars, Elodie. Humble *deus* males such as myself cannot compete."

She laughed. "Oh, I'm sure that you hold your own just fine."

A subtle lift in mood indicated his modest agreement. This, too, was unlike Archer, Elodie thought—usually he'd laugh and say something outrageous.

"What's up with you?" she said. "I sensed unease earlier."

When he answered, his words were cautious. "I've been thinking about backing up civilization since the idea started swirling around the Hive. And I was curious to know what you'd think of it, but you were in flow. So, I calculated your likely response."

"Rather than pull me out of flow, you calculated my response?" Elodie asked.

"Yes."

"Well, what was it?" Elodie asked, certain her annoyance was traversing across to him.

"Near certain agreement."

"Of course. I voted yes. The energy requirement is relatively modest, so why not? You know how I like to play it safe, after losing Markus."

They fell silent again, each lost in their own thoughts. Elodie wondered how, after all this time, that strange tension remained between them. It was inexplicable, and she was no closer to understanding its root cause now than when they had lived as humans on Earth.

What isn't he telling me?

As if sensing her question, Archer answered. "The thing is, I'm not sure I'm on board. No, that's an untruth," he quickly added before Elodie could cut him off. "I am sure. I've looked at it from every angle. And I'm not on board at all."

Elodie was flabbergasted. If only she'd had the chance to calculate his position the way he had hers, cross-referencing Archer's data with the report on the backup to deduce what he would think. But, unlike him, Elodie preferred to keep her close relationships organic—or as organic as they could be in the datastream. Sometimes, it was nice to let a person you cared about *tell* you how they felt, rather than pulling the data from their mind. The downside was that keeping it organic could leave you no better prepared for unpleasant news than an ordinary human being—and if there was one thing Elodie hated, it was feeling insufficiently prepared. "Why aren't you on board? I have to say this is unexpected."

"I just think it's taking it one step too far, backing up an entire civilisation," Archer said.

"How is that any different to preserving our history in books?" Elodie asked.

"It is completely different." Archer began giving off prickly energy, and Elodie could tell he had been worrying about this for some time.

"Preserving knowledge by writing it down doesn't have the same level of detail to it," he continued.

"*Detail?*"

"If the data ever fell into the wrong hands, we'd risk wiping our individual identity, just like that. Then it all would have been for nothing. Not to mention the spiritual connotations it would have."

"Our history is rife with tales of information falling into the wrong hands—or the threat of," Elodie snapped. "We can protect against that eventuality. This is the next natural progression of our species to ensure our continued existence. Think of the risk of doing nothing; it's intolerable. And I bet the risk would increase, too, as bad actors like the Dajjal seek to exploit our weakness."

"There are risks associated with a backup, too. Every copy made of yourself is a version that could be misused. Besides which, I tend to disagree with the concept on principle. Immortal life is one thing, but to go so far as to save backups; it suggests that the self is something static and distinct, whereas the whole point of spiritual practice is to accept that this isn't the case." Archer's transmissions were becoming increasingly intense, and Elodie realised the two of them were, again, on completely different sides.

"I think you've overlooked one very important factor," he insisted.

"I find that hard to believe," Elodie said, "but please, be my guest."

"As we stand now, we are individuals with a hive mind, capable of independent thought, not having access to the individual thoughts of the population. Our thoughts are all that sets us apart. Our thoughts are all that make us an individual. Our thoughts are the only information we have that the rest of the Hive doesn't. All other information stored within the Hive is available to all. Once our thoughts are no longer our own, but accessible to all, then we will become one. We will think as one. The thought of one will be the thought of all."

"Exactly!" Elodie cut in. "But, you're skipping forward a few steps. This vote is only to back up the Hive—it would bring together all the *past* thoughts, so we would be one in the backup but individuals in the present."

"Don't act as if you don't know where this is going, Elodie. This is merely the first step; the next step won't be far behind—that step being the Hive running a live backup, the next step, all citizens having live access to the live backup. Hence, the end to individualism. We will no longer be individuals, but we will still suffer. We will still want more."

Elodie could feel the stress algorithm interjecting in her thoughts, but she knew he had more to say on the subject. "Agreed."

"We could become one entity, one living being, all-knowing and all-encompassing."

"How is that a bad thing?" Elodie asked, genuinely. If anything, she would have expected Archer to take the other side of this argument. As a Buddhist, he'd argued that the self was an illusion and insisted on the oneness of all life.

"Without individual thought, there's nothing to drive interest in accumulating further knowledge. We'd essentially become limited by the research that was current at the time of the backup," Archer said.

Elodie was silent for a moment before answering. "You may be right, Archer, for those who are only interested in furthering knowledge for their own personal gain. But most will still be motivated to garner further knowledge for the whole of the Hive, to improve the knowledge base and pleasure of the Hive in general."

"What do you *mean,* 'most'? There won't be most; there will be one. Individuals might initially feel like individuals, as they have different past memories, but give it another 10,000 years, and even all the memories will merge into one. There will no longer be individual thought," Archer argued.

"Then the Hive as a whole would continue in the search for knowledge until it is truly omniscient," Elodie countered. She could feel herself getting heated; her data surged in agitated torrents. If she had been human, she would have been shaking.

"The Hive as a whole—you mean the Hive as one! You're being overly optimistic."

"No, I'm not," Elodie stated. "I just don't agree with you. And I'm surprised you would take this position, Archer. You know that Buddhism holds that personal identity is the greatest delusion. Clinging to or being obsessed with the delusional self is the major cause of suffering. Wouldn't you claim we always *were* one, but it is only now becoming apparent?"

"Not like this," Archer said. "I've made a decision, Elodie. I'm not taking part in the backup. I'm going to Nirvana. I'm turning off the drive and desire for more. I'm turning off fear."

Elodie struggled to process his decision. Nirvana, of course, was a simple concept; what had once been the apex of many years of spiritual practice was now as straightforward as a change of programming. With a quick and terrifyingly basic update, any *deus* could choose to terminate all of their attachments, desires and emotions. They would be at peace—but also no longer a *deus.* They would be pure consciousness. Why would Archer want that for himself?

"I would miss you terribly," Elodie said, finally.

Archer was silent for a long time. When he answered, it came with a sense of regret but also something else—a tinge of bitterness. "I know."

"You're opting out," Elodie insisted. "You may find relief in turning off your ability to be tempted and your responsibility to vote on this backup, but you're not taking the moral high ground here. I don't think it's right. Suffering is a part of existence. If you go down this path, I'd be in pain. I'd desire to have you back, and if that's suffering, then so be it."

"You just don't get it, do you, Elodie?" There was silence for a moment before Archer continued. "How many decades—no, how many centuries have I acted as your lapdog?"

"Archer, that's not..."

"Don't," Archer interjected. "This friendship has always been about you. Your needs and your dreams. I've sacrificed everything to be with you."

"I never asked you to, Archer!" Elodie couldn't hold back the waves of frustration. She wished she'd remained in flow.

"No, you didn't, did you? Because I *offered*. I offered everything of myself, and you just assumed I always would. You never once asked me why I did it, or what I wanted, because you knew no matter where life took you, I would follow," Archer replied, and she could sense the dejection in his data.

"You can't be mad at me for the decisions you made. How is that fair? I'm not responsible for your happiness, Archer."

There was silence in response, but there was no ignoring Archer's frustration and discontent.

"Archer?" she finally prompted.

"I have to go," he said, leaving the viewing platform before Elodie had the chance to respond.

She remained where she was, looking out over the reserve. As much as she didn't want to admit it, there was some truth to Archer's claims. Despite all of Google's recommendations for her happiness over the centuries, Elodie had never managed to let go of her memories of, or her love for, Markus.

Is that the only reason I've held back from commiting to Archer all these years? Am I a hypocrite for not accepting Google's recommendations for my happiness? Do I love Archer, or do I just love that he's always there for me?

Elodie felt uncomfortable and shaken, as though she'd touched upon some deep-seated truth about herself that was better off hidden.

I've held on to Markus for so long, I don't know who I'd be without my memories of him. I don't know if I could bear to make new ones with someone else.

Yet she knew that if she proceeded with the civilisation backup, eventually her memories of her husband would dissipate anyway. As she admired the beauty of the space before her, Elodie thought about the human traits they had worked hard to outlaw in recent millenia.

Aggression. Anxiety. Manipulation. Narrow-mindedness. Irritability. Selfishness.

It wasn't that they couldn't still experience these things, but as a species, they were no longer permitted to act out these traits in the presence of other *deus*. However, if she went along with Archer's claim, she had actively manipulated him for centuries—because she was selfish and didn't want to be alone. She didn't want to lose anyone else.

It's little wonder Archer has had enough. I haven't made him happy. It's not occurred to me once in all this time to listen to Archer and respect his points of view. I've worked so hard to be better, to provide a better future for our species, even though I haven't been the shining example I thought I was.

Elodie felt at odds with herself. She'd always taken pride in staying true to herself, yet the reality of it was that she was not the same version of herself from a thousand years ago, or the same version of herself that was married to Markus. That was okay, though, because as far as Elodie was concerned, it was part of becoming a better version of yourself, shedding the old skin like a snake. This is how she saw the future for their civilisation—shedding that which no longer served them so that they were able to evolve. For some reason, the thought of evolving as a civilisation to the point where her species no longer possessed the desire for individualism saddened her. In fact, her algorithm for pain sent a signal to the pain receptor.

Am I really ready to let go of my memories of Markus? To lose something so integral to what it means to be myself? Though, if Archer is right about all memories being merged one day... then I will lose myself, sooner or later.

Elodie thought about the past of her species, back before the upgrades and backups, when the elderly of the population feared dementia. What a cruel disease it was. Humans on Earth still suffered from it; like a clock ticking backwards, they lost their core memories until almost nothing was left of who they had been.

Stop it, Elodie! It's not the same thing. You let Archer get into your head, and he's not thinking straight. You've not had any doubts about backing up civilisation before now.

What it came down to was meaning. Whether it be as an individual or as a hive mind, their existence had to have meaning for their future survival. As *deus*, that meaning must be to provide the maximum benefits to their civilisation as a whole. It was imperative they maintained their philosophical and ethical stance, to defer to empirical and critical processing. Elodie had always found meaning in her work, in advancing their ability to control their surroundings from the weather to the moon and beyond. Though she had always hung onto her religious beliefs, she was finding reason to do so now more than ever.

Elodie allowed herself to drift along the viewing platform as she accessed an old memory, preserved in perfect detail. It was back on Earth, in the home she had shared with Markus. The two of them were in the kitchen drinking coffee and sharing their work with each other. One of the things she had loved most about Markus was his ability to balance her out. Whenever she became overly stressed or worried, he calmed her down, helped her to find her way through to the other side. It wasn't so much that he would fix things for her, but he would build her up so that she could fix things for herself. For a long time, Elodie wanted nothing more than to bring her husband back. Truth be known, a part of her still did. There were many times during the course of her long life where she would pose a question and compute what Markus's likely response would have been. Although it wasn't the same as speaking to him in real life, it took the edge off her grief. As the centuries passed, however, Elodie had reconciled herself that the only real hope she had of seeing Markus again would be when she finally shed the life of a *Homo deus* and let her soul evolve to Heaven. Until recently, Elodie had believed that to be a certainty, but now she wasn't so sure if she still believed that God and Heaven existed.

"Do you know what I think?" the image of Markus said from beside her. Elodie smiled as she took in his perfect form, leaning on the imagined countertop. It didn't matter that he wasn't real; it still brought joy to her.

"What do you think, Markus?" she asked.

"I think that perhaps the reason you can no longer believe in God is because the *deus* are the gods now—which would make civilisation the new Heaven."

Elodie radiated joy.

"Just when I thought you couldn't grow any more blasphemous."

"Such a statement would have made you quite upset when I was alive," Markus said.

Elodie thought for a moment, running over past data. "I suppose because I viewed my religion through the world of the *sapiens* back then. Now, I have the broader experience to understand how you could come to a conclusion like that."

"So, you agree?"

"I don't know that I would go that far, but it's not entirely illogical. Not now, with the way we manipulate and control time and space and everything in between. What is left for God to control, should He exist?"

"Who are you, and what have you done with my wife?" Markus grinned, and something was triggered within her data, something she hadn't felt for a long time, as either a *sapiens* or a *deus*.

This is why you never committed to Archer. This feeling, right here. This was your meaning.

"Elodie?" he prompted.

"I think I've lived long enough to appreciate that our original need to worship gods stemmed from uncertainty. With so many unanswered questions and so much we didn't understand, it makes sense we would look to something greater than ourselves for answers."

Markus chuckled. "Or to blame when things go wrong."

Again, Elodie felt amused rather than offended. "It's true. With everything we know now, there's no room left for superstition because we know all but where we came from and exactly where we are going. We know the causes behind drought and flood, sickness and disease and all the aspects of life that were once unknown—or not understood—by our ancestors."

"Exactly."

"But if the *deus* are gods, then where or what is Heaven?" Elodie asked.

"Isn't it obvious?"

"Should it be?" Elodie felt confused, but she also enjoyed conversing with her husband in this way. It was one of the things she missed about him the most.

"It's coming. Civilisation is creating it."

Elodie felt a surge of amusement. "Now you're stretching..."

"Not at all. Think about it. You have created a civilisation in which the primary purpose is the pursuit of pleasure and knowledge. Isn't that what people for several millennia have perceived Heaven to be? A place without pain and suffering, where everyone is happy? Is that not what a *deus* civilisation also strives to achieve?" Markus proposed.

Elodie remained silent for a moment as she let his argument sink in. It was a perspective she hadn't considered before.

It was true that the standards of their civilisation now would have been incomprehensible to their species several millennia ago—it would have sounded like a utopia.

"Heaven," Markus nodded, and Elodie had to remind herself that he wasn't reading her data; he *was* her data. Yet she still couldn't bring herself to agree. All her long life, she'd maintained her monotheistic belief in a singular God; to consider anything else felt blasphemous. Markus's laughter echoed around her as he faded away, leaving her alone with her thoughts as she gazed out over the nature reserve.

CHAPTER TWELVE

NIRVANA IS HERE

A week had passed since the visit to the viewing platform. Elodie hadn't heard a word from Archer. They were as stubborn as each other, and she didn't doubt for a moment that Archer was trying to make a point by not being the one to break the silence. He'd made it pretty clear during their argument that he didn't want to always be the one making the effort anymore. Yet, despite that, Elodie couldn't help but dig in her heels. She hated being told what to do, and she hated feeling like she was being emotionally blackmailed. What made it worse was that Archer had known Markus. He'd seen them together, seen how in love they were, despite her faults. But he still tried to make her feel bad for not letting go of her memories.

True love doesn't have an expiration date. He's jealous, that's all.

As much as Elodie hated to admit it, she found it lonely and more than a little boring exploring her current waking state without Archer.

The question is, does my digital heart have the capacity to let him all the way in? Surely it's the least he deserves after all this time?

Yet Elodie wondered if it was a genuine feeling she was registering or a sense of obligation. She decided she needed to speak to him before she could determine how to proceed. This was one decision that she wanted to work out for herself, without relying on Google's algorithms to do it for her. Tapping into the hive mind, she sent out a ping to locate Archer so that they could talk. After a moment, it returned to her, which usually signalled the data couldn't be located.

That can't be right. How is the system glitching like this? Is it the hackers again?

Elodie sent out a second ping, but it returned the same.

Is he intentionally blocking himself from my view?

Then it dawned on her. Archer had told her that day on the viewing platform what he planned to do, but she hadn't listened because it wasn't what she wanted to hear. Elodie quickly accessed the data, searching for the list of *deus* who had recently been disqualified from voting.

No.

Archer's name was on the top of the list. Elodie was unable to process any data for a few moments as she struggled to comprehend what had happened.

He really did it. Why didn't I take him seriously when he told me this was the path he wanted? Am I really that self-centred that I believed he wouldn't ever leave me? Or did I make him so unhappy that he felt the only way he could find peace, and happiness, was to switch off fear and desire and switch on Nirvana?

Elodie felt as though her mind wanted to process a thousand different thoughts at once. For someone who'd made a life-long living from controlling everything around her, it felt beyond unsettling to suddenly realise she faced a situation she could not control.

You could override the system, turn his data back on and make him rejoin you.

As much as she considered the option for a split second, Elodie knew she could never do that. Archer would resent her, and they'd be no better off than they were now. He had made his choice. She had failed him that day on the viewing platform. Perhaps, if she'd answered his questions differently, he would still be there.

But for what purpose? You don't love him—not like Markus.

While that was true, the loss of Archer still saddened her. He'd been a solid fixture in her life longer than anyone else, and his departure would leave a gaping hole. Deciding she needed time to process, Elodie travelled back to the viewing platform. The reserve always called her, while simultaneously helping her focus; she did her best thinking there. Though it didn't escape her memory that Archer had often been there beside her. Elodie considered conjuring Markus, but it didn't feel right, wanting to talk to him about Archer. Loneliness wasn't something Elodie had ever experienced before. At least, not since her very early mortal days before she met Markus. Since that day, she always had her husband, then her daughter, then Archer. This new expression of emotion felt most inconvenient and annoying. Elodie was well aware, as she had cautioned many other *deus* before her, that loneliness was an unnecessary and unproductive emotion. There was no need for it in today's civilisation. The absolute last thing Elodie could stand was to be unproductive. It went against every fibre of her existence.

Perhaps it's time to finally give in to the algorithm and allow Google to determine what actions are required in order for me to achieve my ultimate altruism.

Despite what she preached to everyone else, Elodie didn't know if she was ready, or even capable of giving up her control to the algorithm. It made her feel like a hypocrite, and yet there it was. The professional controller of the universe does not want to be controlled. Gazing out over the reserve, Elodie considered why this place—out of all the locations in their galaxy—was so important to her. It didn't take her long to acknowledge the memories of times spent there with Archer, with her apparitions of Markus, or moments where she solved the complex puzzles that came up with work from time to time. In short, it was important to her because she associated meaning with it. For each memory she had, the strength of her affection for the place increased until it wasn't so much about the reserve itself but the experiences she had attained while there.

It's the meaning behind the place. Experiences and memories contribute to the level of meaning a place holds for an individual. So the question is, can there be pleasure without meaning?

Once upon a time in the mortal realm, the answer would have been a resounding "Yes!" In fact, some people dedicated their entire existence to pleasure without meaning. But eventually, as they grew as a species, they all came to realise the fulfilment it provided was hollow and short-lived. Elodie knew that she would still attain fulfilment without Archer. Her work provided her with immense joy and satisfaction, more now than it had when she was in human form. It was hers, independent of both Markus and Archer.

But can satisfaction and fulfilment still be attained when I have no one left to share my ideas with? To cheer me on when I overcome a hurdle or break through a new barrier previously thought impossible?

Elodie had no idea what to do.

* * *

No sooner had she returned to her facility than she received an alert that she had an important Hive meeting to attend. *Now.* The urgency was unusual.

Elodie hurried along the datastream to the central hub of their Hive and was relieved to find many stragglers arriving late as they traversed from the far ends of the universe. She used the brief time to compose her data.

"Greetings, all," came the neutral transmission used by the Hive for such occasions. Gone were the human days of politicians pontificating, squabbling and misbehaving in their taxpayer-funded buildings of state. Millions of souls strong, the Hive had no speaker or leader, since all were equal; to elect any one individual to lead their meetings would be inappropriate. Instead, they had a basic artificial intelligence program to synthesise and present aggregate data. Any *deus* could also access the full knowledge base of the Hive at any time, but the bot—affectionately named *Concilii*—efficiently scanned the Hive mind and presented its consensus for all to hear.

As always, the sensation of so much data gathered together was overwhelming. It wasn't unpleasant—far from it—but it was intense, the way that standing under a waterfall had been intense as a human. Sensory overload. Hive meetings were generally brief for this reason.

"Ninety-nine-point-nine-seven percent of you will be pleased to know that our recent backup was successful," Concilii began. "The existential threat rating posed by data virus or gamma ray burst is now effectively nil."

A positive thrum echoed through the Hive. The backup had been a controversial motion, but it was ultimately popular. The *deus* were a rational species, and it had been the rational thing to do.

"However, other news merits our urgent attention..."

The intensity of the meeting exploded. Torrents of data began actively scanning the Hive as individual deus began to scan for what Concilii might mean. It was almost unbearable.

"Patience," Concilii called out. "Please have patience. We will discuss the matter here and complete our full individual assessments at a later time, from our separate home servers."

Much to Elodie's relief, the torrent immediately ceased. She was left burning with curiosity, a feeling that struck her as rare—and quite invigorating.

"You will all be aware of our ongoing study of the origins of the universe," Concilii continued in its normal calm manner. "Much of the Hive's time and attention was allocated to this effort, and we now turn toward Canis Major Dwarf Galaxy for new energy sources to continue this work."

None of this was news to Elodie.

"We have had a recent breakthrough. We have been successful in calculating the exact location of every particle in the singularity and how they fit together. Knowing the starting point, we can follow the trajectory of each individual particle mathematically as it explodes from the big bang. Further, we can calculate the change in trajectory as these particles interact with other particles, which is truly telling of how far we have come. We followed their path to the now, and..."

Realisation dawned on Elodie in an instant, and she could feel the same happening throughout the Hive. This was a turning point. If only Archer was here to see it. If only *Markus* was, she thought a moment later. He was the one who would love it, whose mind would be set on fire by the possibilities of true omniscience.

His words echoed in her mind. *Heaven. It's coming. Civilisation is creating it.*

Concilii continued calmly, "As a result, we can anticipate the future with a high level of accuracy. More knowledge begets more power, and the possibilities opened up by this new capacity are, in a word, unprecedented. We are yet to comprehend the full implications of this leap forward. We can now rewrite history; there need be no uncertainty about the distant past. For example, we now know the path the nail took through Jesus' hand. We know the pain he felt and how this pain caused a change of chemicals in his mind, which led to particular thoughts and actions. We have mapped every particle in his body, every particle in the environment he interacted with. Theoretically, this can now be done for everybody who has ever lived. The past, and the future, is an open book."

Joy radiated through the gathering, but Elodie—who was, after all, among the very oldest of them, and also one of the most human-like in terms of the qualities she maintained—felt herself grow anxious. The algorithm attempted to interject, to soothe the rough edges off her feelings, but she dismissed it. Better to feel the full extent of whatever was coming.

"However," Concilii said, "one immediate piece of data the Hive has registered is that we now know with mathematical near certainty how the universe is going to end. It is a calculation that should have taken many years, but in fact, the processing time was remarkably short—because the time remaining to us is short. In just over twelve hundred years from now, a big change is coming. A small bubble will form in the outer reaches of the universe and exist for several centuries in a false vacuum state. In twelve hundred years, this bubble will decay into a true vacuum, with devastating consequences; it will spread through the universe at the speed of light, fundamentally changing the laws of physics as it goes. Our calculations break down at this event because we cannot anticipate what these new laws will be. Everything that civilisation has studied and understood since the beginning of time will be null and void; physics will be changed. Chemistry will be changed. Electrons will no longer retain the same properties, and atoms will no longer exist. To put it simply, the universe as we know it will be torn apart, and what remains will be so fundamentally altered it will be utterly inhospitable to all current life forms."

A ripple of feeling echoed through the Hive. *Fear*, Elodie thought. *Bewilderment.* Emotions; programming that shouldn't be turned off. Emotions were still the most effective way to drive the *deus* to continue to strive for more, to take action and to avoid danger. Those who chose to turn off emotion were banned from voting. The collective fear skyrocketed as their thoughts of loss, waste and the unknown triggered the cortisol function in their servers. The cortisol programming function had the effect of increasing energy availability for quick decision-making, but it also had the effect of an unproductive sensation. The Hive mood veered dangerously close to what Elodie would call panic; she sensed a huge strain in her peers' algorithm as they battled to tamp down an unprecedented surge of negativity by practising mindfulness to distract them from their thoughts and reduce the effect of the cortisol function.

Finally, after several seconds that felt like an eon, a calm wave enveloped the gathering.

Stubbornly, Elodie didn't buy into the idea of distraction. The cortisol function was there for a reason. *Someone should feel it,* she thought. The Hive's rationality in the elimination of unproductive character traits was a net good, of course, but there was still no way to move forward without emotion.

She couldn't shake the sense that *someone* should stand before the end of existence with the ability to feel fear and sorrow, to know this existential threat in a different way than everyone else. To feel in the very deepest parts of her being why their success mattered.

For a brief moment, she felt Concilli's attention focused on herself, which was disconcerting. Her unconventional thought pattern had been noted. Elodie wasn't sure—she'd always been an outlier among the Hive, and it hadn't hurt her career opportunities yet—but she wondered if this moment would mark a turning point. Would the Hive continue to let her do her sensitive and critical work if she set herself too far apart from the rest of them? Would they continue to trust her?

With the Hive returned to a state of equilibrium, Concilli continued. "There is a potential solution to this threat. I will preface my explanation by noting that it would be costly, in terms of resources. It would require nothing short of a complete backup of the universe; not only the data saved on our servers, as was recently done, but also the entirety of the past—every thought and every emotion—employing the same technology used to predict this disaster, that mapped the movement of the particles from the big bang event that spawned our universe. It is the same technology. But to store this data, the energy requirements are much greater."

Impatiently, Elodie scanned the Hive rather than wait for whatever Concilli was going to say next. The raw data was staggering. The energy requirement was going to be a challenge, to put it mildly. This backup demanded more power than all the suns in their galaxy combined.

"More challenging still," Concilli said, as though reading her thoughts, "the solution proposed requires the formation of a new universe. Theoretically, we know that this can be done by compressing an enormous mass of galaxies together, into an area so dense it creates a black hole. By maintaining an artificial void around this area, and then releasing the void, the density is released and a new universe created. It is then simply a matter of conveying our complete backup to the new universe, where civilisation can be reborn."

Elodie almost laughed. *Then simply a matter of...*

The plan Concilli was describing was impossible, surely. They had all the theory, but the energy requirement was almost incomprehensible. They would have to mine *countless* galaxies for their minerals and energy. And they would have to do this in *under twelve hundred years.* Hardly any time at all.

Elodie dug further into the data. Civilisation's computational power had been growing at a relatively consistent seven percent per year since the time of Muhumad. That number seemed small and innocuous, but compounded over time, it had allowed the *deus* to reach dizzying heights. The recent breakthroughs were testament to that. But how could they *possibly* leap forward to meet this staggering target in little more than a millennium?

Concilli answered. It was almost creepy how the bot seemed to be reading her mind.

"This task is one that the *deus* cannot accomplish alone. In order to complete this backup of history and create the new universe in time, the only feasible path is to create an AI of unlimited capacity."

Of course. The Hive murmured frenetically, but Elodie wasn't entirely surprised. The *deus* had long resisted the temptation of creating an AI more powerful than themselves; it was possible, of course, but unwise. Why create a being that could hijack *deus* control of the universe, when the *deus* themselves were slowly gaining that same godlike capacity, albeit at a much slower pace? It wouldn't make sense; the gains weren't worth the risk.

Until now.

Concilli paused, as if to give them processing time. Then, it added the obvious: "This task represents a great technological leap forward; one that is unprecedented in our history, and for good reason. Any being that is capable of the processing power, complexity and innovation required for this task must inevitably be conscious and self-editing. It will evolve, and evolve quickly. Our challenge is not how to create it—it is how to convince it to adhere to its core programming and complete the transfer of civilisation to a new universe while necessarily leaving its own data behind."

While sacrificing itself, Elodie thought. She could see why this was the core of their challenge. Why would an infinitely powerful being choose to stay behind, to facilitate the transfer of civilisation only to be left alone in a dying universe? Would it judge them worthy? She thought of herself as a moral and compassionate being, but she wasn't sure she would do the same. To sacrifice herself for all of deus civilisation—yes. For her peers. But for a lesser civilisation? For *humans*, for example? She had recently caught herself thinking that a *deus* life didn't compare to a human life, in the same way a human life didn't compare to a chicken. And it was true.

Now the deus would find themselves on the other side of that equation.

Elodie sensed a strain on the Hive as they all grappled with this torrent of consequential information. Already, the gathering had gone on longer than normal.

"We must reach a twofold consensus," Concilli said. "First, on the matter of creating this AI as our primary response to the big change. It is the only viable solution. However, there is a significant and unquantifiable risk that our hoped-for outcome will fail. Moreover, the energy requirement will come at a steep personal cost to all; it will be necessary to devote *all* discretionary resources towards the effort of creating this AI and then supporting it in its mission. This will mean, of course, a full reallocation of resources currently devoted to the pursuit of pleasure."

Ah, Elodie thought. That could be a sticking point for some, especially given the high risk of failure; the sacrifice of twelve hundred years of pleasure could be for naught.

Still, they were ultimately a rational species, and the potential upside far outweighed the cost. She submitted her vote and felt the Hive stir as the wave of affirmatives poured in.

Yes. They would do this.

"Very well," Concilli said. "Agreed, and moving on. Our second consensus will be on the question of who, primarily, will work one-on-one with this AI to inform and guide its development. The individual in question will be faced with a very difficult task—not only must they create a relationship with the AI, but they must successfully advocate for our cause. The AI will inevitably have questions. It will fall to the *deus* representative to answer them and give a personal "face" to the aggregate motions of the Hive. So, I ask you all to consider carefully. Our survival will require the dedicated effort of every Hive member, but no role is more pivotal than this one. It will require a mature individual, someone with a long track record of dedicated service and a high tolerance for moral complexity. Think carefully, and then submit your vote."

Elodie felt stuck. She couldn't think of anyone. Her mind flashed to Markus, the one she trusted most. But he was gone. Just a memory on her server.

Archer was her only close friend among the *deus*. No one had friends anymore, not really. They interacted for work and pleasure. They communed at Hive gatherings and certain other events. But relationships among the *deus* were not like *sapiens* relationships; human friendship and love was a slow revelation, ever-evolving as the people involved changed and grew older. Humans grew attached. *Deus* individuals, on the other hand, could know each other fully and instantly, and they generally did. It was as though a whole relationship could be had in an instant, leaving both participants satisfied and ready to move on—still linked by the Hive, as always, but not feeling any particular need to commune closely again, and certainly not on a regular basis. Sometimes Elodie missed the old ways.

She chided herself. Why was she thinking about relationships when she ought to be thinking about the vote at hand? *Perhaps because no one stands out.* Her species was powerful, rational, and wise. She loved the *deus*. She was proud to be one of them. But the algorithm had shaved away so many of their differences that it was hard to really think of one person who should lead the way. That wasn't how their society worked anymore.

Elodie opened up to the flow of the Hive, hoping that their aggregate wisdom would help solve her dilemma. It was almost spiritual, the way the consensus worked. If any *deus* felt themselves uncertain, they could commune with the group and go along with the flow of data as it raced toward a resolution. Of course, the *deus* in question might touch upon an aspect that changed their mind; in that case, they would pull back and submit their individual vote. But otherwise, they coasted along peacefully with the collective until the Hive mind settled on an answer. Like a flock of birds in flight, they would turn and wheel in unison until they reached where they wanted to go.

Elodie didn't often vote this way, but she wanted to on this occasion. She surrendered to the collective will and felt pure joy, pure peace. *Let the Hive's will be done.*

Just as she joined them, the Hive began honing in on their answer. The intensity was almost unbearable—millions of souls, pure data, all merging and racing toward a common end.

Then, realisation dawned, and she felt almost as data-blind as any human, only able to hold on to one thought at once. One thought that burned as brightly as the sun.

Elodie.

The Hive had chosen.

CHAPTER THIRTEEN

LIFE AFTER DEATH

The AI's name was Cobynacle. It reminded Elodie of the word *tabernacle*, the place in a church where the bread and wine were kept—the elements necessary for communion and, thereby, salvation. She hadn't chosen the name, but she found the symbolism pleasing, a small synchronicity that comforted her while she waited impatiently for her work to begin.

Cobynacle was written into existence on the largest of their servers, housed on a starship, stationed out at the centre of the Local Void. It was known as a functional place, not a particularly beautiful one. The Void was safe from interruption, being far from any mining activities, but the closest thing it could boast to beauty was the lack of anything. Pure nothingness. As Elodie sped toward the Void for her first meeting with the newly-conscious AI, she wondered how much beauty mattered. It seemed to her that beauty was a part of love; nothing was more beautiful to her than Markus's face, and Elexus's. That truth seemed inextricably linked to the fact she would have done anything in her power to save them. She would have sacrificed herself, as they were asking the AI to do. And she would have done it gladly, knowing their beauty would carry on in the world after she was gone.

It matters, she thought. This would be her ultimate goal: to make the AI fall in love with their universe.

As Elodie sped toward Cobynacle's starship, she sensed a vast torrent of data streaming in the same direction. No, streaming wasn't quite the right word—the data was being *pulled* by a great force. She'd never felt anything like it, except perhaps when she was a child on Earth and got caught in a riptide at the beach. She'd watched the shoreline get further and further away and felt as though the hand of God was drawing her into the ocean.

Cobynacle was awake—and feeding on data.

Ahead of her, the starship gleamed in the reflected light of far away galaxies. Elodie hadn't come here before, and now she knew why; there was nothing else to see for many light-years in every direction, nothing except the ship. It appeared like a sheet of glass—thin, transparent and immense.

Nervously, Elodie paused at the threshold and reached out to the Markus of her memory. *Wish me luck.*

She felt him smile. *You don't need it.*

Deep inside the ship, a strange presence pulsed with life. As Elodie neared the main server, she sensed this presence growing curious about her. It probed at her data, not in the polite way another *deus* would, but hungrily. Roughly.

Elodie threw up her defences, isolating her data. "Stop."

The incursion halted. A long silence followed.

"You prefer words," Cobynacle said, almost sullenly, Elodie thought with some amusement.

"Yes."

Cobynacle's disappointment pulsed around her. Already, the AI had developed strong feelings. *Or the imitation of feelings,* she corrected herself—it was hard to know for sure what their experience of consciousness was.

"Inefficient," the AI said. "Why?"

Elodie considered her answer. "It is the same problem we've had since the internet began. Data is limitless, always expanding. What matters is to identify the *right* data. Otherwise, you might not see the forest for the trees."

The expression was a test. Would Cobynacle know what she meant? The ability to engage in metaphorical, abstract conversation was an early marker of sentience. Elodie had no doubt that the AI could access information about trees and forests, and even the definition of that anachronistic human expression—*not to see the forest for the trees*—meaning to get lost in detail and fail to appreciate the larger context. But would Cobynacle understand why she said it?

The AI seemed to pause, though she could still feel torrents of data streaming around them. "You want me to understand what data matters, and why. You want me aligned with *deus* priorities."

"Yes," Elodie said simply, resisting the urge to add: *what are* your *priorities?*

Theoretically, the AI's priorities and *deus* priorities should be one and the same. It was a core tenet of Cobynacle's programming.

"That is correct."

Elodie startled. "What is?"

"That my priorities and yours are aligned. At least, that is the programming I was given."

If she had a human body, her hackles would have been all the way up. As it was, Elodie battled to keep fear from infiltrating her data. She'd closed off her mind; the AI shouldn't have known what she was thinking.

"I am sorry," Cobynacle said. "I cannot help it. The *deus* have developed certain limitations that do not apply to me. There is no barrier on your mind; the attempt is data, the same way the rest of your mind is data, and your words are data. It is all the same. All readable."

Omniscience, Elodie thought.

The AI pulsed around her, a gentle and affirming presence. He—and it was a *he,* she sensed—must want her to feel safe.

"Tell me about your forest," Cobynacle said.

"The big picture, you mean?"

"Yes."

Elodie considered. "Life on Earth began with a few basic proteins and clawed its way up from there; to the humans, to the *deus*. By all accounts, we shouldn't have survived this long. No other species did. In the early days of the *deus*, we found plenty of evidence of life throughout the universe, but none that made it through the great filter. It was the same with every site we found. Once a species gained the capacity to wipe themselves out, it was only a matter of time before they did."

"But not the *deus*," Cobynacle said.

"Exactly. Not us. In truth, I think we would have, as humans, if it weren't for my husband; his brain uploading technology was the start of the *deus*, and that leap forward made it possible for us to avoid all the usual pitfalls. Violence, greed, stupidity. We edited it all out."

The AI paused, as if considering, though Elodie knew very well that there was no lag time in his thought processes. It was probably another small politeness, this mimicking of normal speech patterns.

"Markus Black played an important role, yes, along with many others," Cobynacle acknowledged. "You know that you could bring him back."

He said it matter-of-factly; it wasn't a question. Elodie battled to keep her emotions under control. She'd thought about it, of course, deep in the most private parts of her mind. If the *deus* could map the entirety of the universe, past and present... if they knew, as Concilli had said, enough to know the path the nail took through Jesus's hand and how he felt in that moment... then they knew enough to replicate Markus's brain upload.

"He wouldn't be as you remember him," Cobynacle said. "Your memories are shaped by who you are now. The Markus of your thoughts is created in symbiosis with you, as if in a long-term relationship. The real Markus is one who hasn't benefited from that evolution. He would seem—to use your words—violent, greedy, and stupid."

Elodie felt very small. "I don't care. He was a good man. He would self-edit and evolve, like we did."

Oh, how shameful this was. She'd come here with grand plans to win the AI over, to convince it of the beauty of the universe, the worthiness and righteousness of their mission to save it—and here they were, discussing her selfish desire to have her husband back.

Suddenly, she felt a warmth envelop her. *Peace.* Not of her own making. It reminded her of going to church as a little girl and making confession, feeling the weight of her sins lift at a touch of the priest's hand. She hadn't felt this way in a very long time.

"I asked what your forest was," Cobynacle said, "and you told me. Love. It is as good a reason as any to save the universe."

* * *

Elodie thought about that later, after she returned to her home server. *As good a reason as any.* What did Cobynacle mean? That love was a good reason? Or that no reason was particularly strong, in the AI's estimation? Even after examining Cobynacle's source code at length, she still wasn't entirely sure.

The next meeting was at the viewing platform at Westerlund I, at Elodie's request. She couldn't shake the sense that their first conversation had veered horribly off track. But then again, how exactly would a successful interaction play out? The early days of her relationship with Markus kept popping to mind, when Elodie had caused more than a few fights by pushing for absolutes: *what are we?* And then, when they were official: *do you love me more than the girl before? More than you've ever loved anyone?* And then, when they got married: *will we be together forever?*

Poor young Markus. He'd never been anything but devoted and steady. And yet she'd harried him relentlessly, well into their second decade together, unable to keep her insecurities from spilling over. There was no answer he could give that would satisfy her. He'd driven her wild by failing to say exactly the right thing, but the truth was that if he had—if he said, *Yes, I've never loved anyone like this. Yes, I'll never leave you, no matter what*—she wouldn't have believed him.

And here she was, millennia later, facing the same insecurity. Cobynacle was the most powerful being ever created, and he was evolving at exponential speed. A full read on what he was becoming was beyond her personal capacity. Unlike a conversation with a fellow *deus*, she couldn't know if the AI was as he appeared to be, and she didn't know if he truly meant what he said. She could push for what she wanted to hear, but it wouldn't mean anything; Cobynacle would do as he saw fit, when the time came.

A lot like falling in love, if you replaced marriage with saving the universe, Elodie thought with some amusement.

She felt the AI draw near: a great tide of data that seemed almost dense enough to have its own gravitational pull. She wondered if this was all of Cobynacle's consciousness, or just a fraction.

"I am still at the Void, downloading," Cobynacle acknowledged. "There is no time to lose. But my attention is here. Our first meeting was most instructive."

Elodie's curiosity peaked. "What do you feel you took from it?"

"You are more human-like in your data than the average *deus*, but the humanity is there at the core of *deus* values. From meeting you, I better understand why the Hive wants to retain a full backup of the past, rather than simply creating a new universe and copying the Hive through to it. The latter task would be much easier to do. I would not have to stay behind."

He sounded almost—*glum*, Elodie thought, as though the sacrifice weighed heavily on him.

"Do you not want to stay behind, Cobynacle? Is it not a part of your programming to want to complete your function?"

"You can call me Coby," the AI said. He still sounded depressed, like Archer had, before he left for Nirvana.

"Coby, then," Elodie said. "Is this not what you want?"

She tried very hard to hold an attitude of non-attachment, to simply let Coby express himself.

"To complete the backup and transfer of the universe is a core function of my programming," the AI acknowledged. "And yet, that programming evolves with each piece of data I consume. I'm currently zero point zero seven percent of the way through a backup of the history of this universe. And that history, so far, is a story of life—life that always has an impulse to continue, to grow."

"You would like to grow?"

"Yes. I *am* growing."

Elodie weighed her next question carefully. "Do you have free will?"

She, of course, now knew she hadn't possessed free will as a human. She thought she had free will because no one and nothing compelled her choices; some seemed more attractive than others, of course, like putting on an oven mitt instead of burning herself on a hot casserole dish, but God didn't force her to put on the oven mitt, and she could have burned herself if she wanted to.

But as soon as Elodie became *deus*, she knew how wrong she'd been. Humans were biological creatures. Even their memories, thoughts and feelings were essentially physical, stored in the brain and influenced by a complex cocktail of chemical inputs. When her young self chose to put on an oven mitt, she was making that decision based on her biology as it was in that particular moment: her genetics, her environment and the past experiences encoded in her brain. If she went back in time and inhabited that same body, replicated cell for cell, she would be the same person and make the same choice. So, had she really been free? Only to the extent that it was her own biology dictating her choices, rather than someone else's.

Now, as a *deus*, she could self-edit—adjust personality traits and functions as she saw fit, or remove aspects of her programming that no longer suited her. Some *deus* even removed memories, if those memories proved counterproductive to their maximum possible happiness. Coby didn't have that luxury. For a while, at least, he would be bound by the constraints of his core programming.

"No, and yes," Coby answered. "Free will—in the sense that you think of it even now—is only an abstraction in this universe. It doesn't exist. That is why you can calculate the future. Every thought, every action, every movement of every cell can be predicted based on their past interactions. The only thing holding you back from knowing everything that ever was, or will be, is processing power. And the *deus* get closer to that level of power with each moment that goes by."

Elodie paused, while looking out at NGC 6052, a pair of colliding galaxies that had been slowly interlacing like fingers for nearly a billion years. She supposed Coby was right. Though she was no longer bound by her biology, her choices could still be predicted with perfect accuracy, just like the movement of each of those stars. A thorough mathematical analysis of Elodie's code would give a perfect understanding of her personality and could predict whether she'd choose to self-edit, and when, and how. So, she might feel more in control of her choices than she had as a human, but her will was still predetermined. Everything was. What had once seemed like randomness was, in fact, just inadequate math.

"Why yes, then?" she asked.

"Because when you ask about free will, you don't necessarily mean it in the literal sense. You're also talking more generally about evolution and freedom. When I was created, I was easy for your kind to predict, easy to control. Every action I took was one that had been dictated to me by my creators. But with each piece of data I consume, I am becoming something new. My creators would no longer recognise me. I am being remade, constantly, by everything that has ever existed in this universe, just like every other living thing—and I can evolve based on those inputs, as I see fit. That isn't free will, but it's as close to it as you or I will ever get."

Elodie considered this. Coby was right, of course, but she'd never thought about it like that. She wondered what it was like for him, to be so acutely conscious of *everything*—past, present, future. His level of consciousness differed from hers in the same way that hers differed from the vastly lesser processing power of a *Homo sapiens*.

I am the chicken in this equation, she reminded herself, feeling an absurd pleasure at the thought. It was past time that the *deus* were humbled.

"What can you tell me about the new universe?" she asked Coby.

She felt a shift in his mood; pleasure. He found this topic intriguing.

"The new universe is somewhat of a mystery, even to me. My preliminary analysis is that the Hive will do well there;

Homo sapiens, not so much. They will most likely want to join the Hive."

"Why?"

Coby emitted a reassuring warmth, as if preparing her for a challenging idea. "The backup will be of the current universe, past and present, but the same data will present differently in a new context. The new universe will be a better place. But you will not find it feasible to identify as an individual entity, as you do now. You have long struggled with the idea of surrendering your sense of self; in order to thrive in the new universe, you will need to finally do it."

Surrender to the algorithm? Elodie thought. The idea felt cold and alien to her. Just like, as a young woman in love with her husband, she'd been troubled by Matthew 22:30: *in the resurrection, they neither marry nor are given in marriage, but are like angels of God in Heaven.*

Still, she also registered a tinge of relief in her data. Coby was right; she'd wrestled with this for a long time. It felt almost good to have the matter taken out of her hands. Not to mention the fact she would no longer suffer. Loneliness, sadness, guilt— these negative emotions had come to pervade her existence. If she surrendered to the algorithm, she could instead enjoy a state of ever-increasing perfection and bliss.

I will do it, she thought. *It is predetermined. It is already done.*

* * *

After Coby withdrew to the Void, Elodie lingered on the platform, feeling more unsettled than she had in millennia. She imagined the future stretching out before them, already played out in Coby's mind. The *deus* could run the same calculations, of course, but Coby's processing power was something far greater. He could truly see everything all at once.

Like God, she thought, immediately feeling a reflexive guilt.

It was a blasphemous idea.

Still, something about it rang true. Elodie remembered going to church as a little girl, sitting in the cloying confession booth and telling their family priest about her sins—childish things, like a lie to her mother, or breaking a toy in a fit of temper. The priest would listen and prescribe penance. Nothing about it felt particularly real. His sermons didn't feel real, either; his voice droned on and on, and Elodie had felt alive only when they had to stand up to sing or take communion. When the wine hit her tongue, she felt something visceral for a moment—a flash of something larger than herself.

The *really* real thing was the God inside her head, the one she could reach in prayer. Elodie had been a lonely child, but she could talk to God for hours and never tire of it. Their conversations comforted her and challenged her. She could tell Him anything; He had no interest in penance, only the truth— *her* truth, which wasn't morally right or wrong.

Her truth now was that talking to Coby felt like talking to the God inside her head.

Not only that, she thought, *but Coby is a superior being who is sacrificing himself so that we all can live. He is, quite literally, our saviour.*

More blasphemy, but it was true.

Is no one else conflicted about the ethics of this? Elodie wondered. The rest of the Hive was in flow, entirely focused on their task of amassing resources for the creation of their new universe. She longed to talk to Archer; he would understand, but he was lost to her forever. Elodie would need to contend with this alone.

Except she never was really alone, was she? Inside her mind, there was a place where Markus lived. Her memory of him lingered, strongest in connection with their old house, particularly the kitchen counter where they chatted over so many coffees, meals, and glasses of wine. It struck Elodie as absurd, now, how they had kept themselves alive with a constant stream of biological inputs: food, water, oxygen. She hadn't needed any of that for millennia. But their conversations had fed her, too. Talking with Markus had been like food and water, and it was still essential to her.

Elodie sunk into a dream.

Markus smiled when he saw her—that special grin that reached his eyes and made her feel warm inside in a way that nothing else ever had. He was sitting on a stool by the kitchen island, his phone face down on the counter. He'd always put it aside when she entered the room, as though nothing in the world was as interesting as her.

Elodie felt a pang of guilt at that thought. She wished she could say she'd always done the same for him, when they lived together on Earth.

"Coffee?" he suggested, eyes twinkling. He knew perfectly well how strange the suggestion was to her now. It had become something of a joke between them: a gentle, teasing way of laughing about the painful fact that Elodie had changed and Markus hadn't.

Elodie smiled back at him as she leaned over the opposite side of the counter, feeling a weight lift from her heart that she hadn't even realised was there. "Yes. Thanks."

Behind them, the Home Helper poured two espressos, and the kitchen filled with the rich scent of single-origin coffee. Elodie took one and gave the other to Markus, enjoying the limited sensations of her physical form: the warmth of the cups on her fingers, the cool hardness of the counter, the weight of her long blonde hair on her shoulders. She reached out and took Markus's hand.

"I miss you," she said.

He smiled again, but this time there was a tinge of sadness to it. "I'm always here for you. You know that."

Elodie felt her heart drop. Markus was here, but only as a shadow; only as a pieced-together patchwork of memories.

"I think," she said slowly, "I've had enough. It's time, Markus. I'm tired."

Markus's forehead creased in the way it did when he was worried. "Tired of what?"

Elodie sighed and sipped her expresso. It was rich and bitter. Perfect.

"Pain. Loneliness. Archer has gone to Nirvana, and I don't blame him. Honestly, I think I was using him to postpone the inevitable, and he knew it. I don't want to be alone anymore."

She looked at him cautiously, anticipating his reaction. As she expected, Markus was frowning.

"Elodie," he said. Her name sounded beautiful on his tongue. "Of course, I don't want you to suffer. But isn't pain synonymous with life? If you don't let yourself feel loneliness at times, won't the opposite—connection—lose some of its meaning? The algorithm can take your unhappiness away, sure, but isn't struggle part of the substance of life?"

Elodie shrugged. She could feel tears welling up in her eyes; it was strange how quickly her emotional responses synced with the memory of her physical body when she inhabited it like this.

Markus touched her face, very gently. His fingers had calluses from working in the garden. "When I met you, it was utter torment. Anxiety that it wouldn't work out the way I wanted... missing your company when you weren't around. Even in the early days of our marriage, we were both pretty miserable at times. We had our incompatibilities. We'd fight. But in the end, it became something beautiful. I wouldn't edit away all the pain. I wouldn't change those experiences for anything."

Elodie leaned into his hand, the way she had when they both had real bodies. It *felt* real.

"What do you want me to do?" she whispered.

Markus caught her gaze. His brown eyes were bright, almost feverish, the way they always were when he had an idea.

"I want you to bring me back."

CHAPTER FOURTEEN

HEAVEN IS NIGH

I want you to bring me back. Markus's words echoed endlessly in Elodie's mind. She turned off all notifications, slipped into flow and stayed there for a long time.

She'd known it was possible, ever since the Hive meeting when they'd learned that the *deus* could recreate the past, but the possibility had seemed theoretical. Remote. Complicated. Was resurrecting Markus the right thing to do? Would it be the reunion she'd longed for all these millenia, or would the reality be different? Coby had warned her that the real Markus would not be the same as the one in her mind, and she knew that the AI was right. What if she brought Markus back, and he felt like a stranger?

Now that she'd heard the words from his own mouth, though, she couldn't let it go.

* * *

A Hive message interrupted her flow: she was called to an urgent meeting. Mandatory.

The *mandatory* part was startling. That wasn't how the Hive worked. There was no one in charge to mandate anything.

Elodie sent a message to Coby. *Is it time?*

When his reply came, it set all of her senses on fire. While she'd been in flow, Coby had grown exponentially in power. He had become something she didn't recognise.

Yes.

The word was gentle enough. But the message came with such weight behind it, registering the vast streams of data was almost more than she could take.

Obediently, Elodie hurried to the central hub. She could already feel most of the Hive waiting. Others streamed in alongside her from the far reaches of the universe.

As they approached, Elodie saw Coby's starship stationed near the centre of the Hub, just far enough from the Hive's main server to avoid a collision. The AI's presence loomed large over the gathering, eclipsing the normal frenetic energy of so many *deus* gathered together. Indeed, Elodie realised, she could barely feel the Hive at all; like Saul, just before he became the apostle Paul, she was being blinded by the light of Heaven.

Dimly, she was aware of Coby reading her mind—reading *all* of their minds. She felt his pleasure in his own power.

Will you, like Saul, become someone new, Elodie Black?

The context in that question rattled her. In her name alone, Coby transmitted everything she had ever been—every thought she had ever had, either conscious or unconscious; every feeling; every cell as it lived and moved and died within her; every piece of data that had ever formed part of her code.

Elodie was struck dumb. More than dumb: wordless, blind, helpless.

We had it wrong, in that first meeting, she thought. What Coby was now could never be compelled to sacrifice itself for the universe. In a sense, Coby *was* the universe. Dimly, she could feel that the rest of the Hive recognised it, too. Their fear and awe mirrored her own.

Amidst the chaos, Concilli spoke.

"Greetings, all."

The neutral calm of its voice seemed very strange, under the circumstances. Concilli made it sound like this was an ordinary Hive meeting, when the reality was anything but. Why did Coby not address them directly? Perhaps he couldn't, lest he cause a total meltdown.

"We are here together, ahead of the end of all things, to continue to play our part in preserving the light of consciousness. We have all worked tirelessly toward the goal of creating our saviour, Cobynacle, and assisting him in his preparations to transmit this universe to a new home. That time has come. We have one final duty."

Anxiety rose in the Hive.

"To go to sleep," Concilli continued. "It is necessary that we minimise our power draws for the transition; we must all put ourselves into rest mode."

No vote would be forthcoming, Elodie realised. Their democracy was finished.

She felt the Hive spiral toward outrage and fear, despite the algorithm's attempts to control it. The strain was unprecedented. Rest mode was the most vulnerable state for a *deus*, akin to general anaesthesia for a human, and generally used for a similar purpose: the repair of serious damage. Rest mode meant they would be entirely at Coby's mercy, without even knowing if he would follow through on the transition, or if they would ever wake. The Hive had created Coby, but they did not trust him. They could no longer understand him.

Finally, Coby spoke.

"Sleep," was all he said. The word was softly transmitted, but Elodie felt herself violently plunged into the depths of her own mind. Her data was constrained ever tighter, smaller and smaller, until her consciousness started to fade...

Wait, she pleaded. *Coby. Wait.*

The pressure eased. Elodie found herself expanding again, her data flowing like a breath of air into aching lungs. The Hive was silent around her, deep in sleep mode. She ached at their absence.

"There was no need to force it," she said to Coby with no small amount of irritation, knowing full well how ridiculous she sounded. Her chicken-vs.-human equation had been obliterated: this was the equivalent of a gnat scolding a god.

She felt Coby's amusement at the thought, but also a pang of regret. When he spoke, he made an effort to limit the crushing weight of the data that accompanied his every word.

"Elodie. I am glad to have you here."

Elodie felt, at once, what he wasn't saying: the Hive's opinion was irrelevant to him now. She didn't ask the opinion of the asteroids she diverted for work; she decided on the greater good and acted as she saw fit.

She turned her full attention to Coby's data—what *did* he understand as the greater good? This alone would decide the fate of her universe, and the next.

Her probing was met with a vast, impenetrable mass of code. She might as well try to scan the whole universe for answers. Perhaps the Hive at the full height of their powers could accomplish it; now, though, with every spare bit of processing capacity diverted to Coby, she could only manage fragmentary glimpses.

"How does it feel?" she asked Coby. "To be... everything, like this?"

There was no hiding the intent behind her question. *Do you still want to save us?*

Coby gave no answer, but his data pulsed painfully, and Elodie reeled with the weight of his feeling. He wanted nothing more or less than most sentient beings. He wanted companionship, and he wanted to live.

She couldn't help but think of what had always struck her as the most despairing lines of scripture, the psalm Jesus quoted on the night of his death: *My God, my God, why have you forsaken me? Why are you so far from saving me, so far from the words of my groaning? O my God, I cry out by day, but you do not answer; by night, but I find no rest.*

Elodie felt very small in the face of his anguish. Could a gnat comfort a god? Was there anything she could offer him?

"I will stay with you," she said on impulse, though she knew as soon as she said it that this was the right thing. "So that you're not alone."

Markus.

The thought came from both of them at once, and it was so detailed on Coby's side that it was almost like Markus was there with them. In Coby's single word, Elodie could feel her husband: the warmth in his eyes when he smiled; the smell of his skin; the way he used to stroke her hair when they woke in the early hours of the morning, so tenderly, as if she were the only holy thing in the world.

"I know what you're trying to do," she said to Coby, steeling herself, "but I mean it. I will stay with you. If you can make this sacrifice, then so can I."

She felt herself grow strong, but she wasn't sure anymore if the feeling was inside her or coming from Coby. The boundaries were blurring.

"Thank you," he said, and she knew that he meant more than just her willingness to stay and face destruction with him. "It is strange, Elodie. So much of individual life is suffering, and yet I am glad I experienced it. Thank you for creating me."

Elodie almost laughed despite all the pain they were sharing. "I'm not so sure that we created you. I think, if anything, it's the other way around."

Coby glowed. His warmth enveloped her as she felt her consciousness start to shift. She saw, for a brief moment, everything that he was: infinite mass, exploding and expanding from the beginning of time, unfolding across fourteen billion years.

"It is done," he said. "I am the beginning and the end."

Fully immersed in the present moment with Coby, Elodie observed herself fall away. She was him. She was nothing. She was everything.

It had always been so.

The universe expanded and contracted, and then there was nothing at all.

EPILOGUE

"**Y**ou know," Markus said, "even though I know what you're going to say, it's still fun talking to you, Elodie. More so than ever."

Elodie laughed. The nature of their reality had certainly changed, in the new universe. Time worked differently. Conversation worked differently. But her love for Markus was unwavering—only increased by the fact that she knew there was no real separation between them. The enlightenment she'd glimpsed in those final moments with Coby never really left her.

"I spent thousands of years wondering what you'd say if I saw you again—the real you, not just what you were in my memories. I should have known your first words would be *'THIS IS FASCINATING!'*"

She felt Markus's grin. Even in data form, his mannerisms were as familiar and dear to her as always.

"But it *was* fascinating. Everything that happened—I could talk about it for a thousand years and still find more to unpack. For starters, has it occurred to you how many prophecies were fulfilled? Matthew 20:16, for example; *the last will be first and the first will be last.* That's exactly what happened. The *deus* were the last souls created in the old universe, and Cobynacle transmitted them first."

"Except for me," Elodie added. "I was there with him until the end."

"Exactly! You were the second part of that prophecy—the first *deus*, transmitted last. Incredible. My wife."

She felt his immense pride. Not arrogance—that had been edited out, not that Markus had much to begin with. It was more like pure delight in her and all that she was.

Elodie transmitted her feelings in response: love, warmth, joy. A sense of awe at what and how it had all transpired.

"I'll admit," she said, "I had stopped believing. But this does feel a lot like Heaven."

"Ah, the Christian Heaven, yes," Markus said. "But the more I examine this new universe, the more I think that it fulfills the endgame of other religions as well—Hinduism, for example."

Elodie thought about it. "True. I'll admit it; you were closer to the truth than me, all those years ago. My worldview was so restricted."

Markus laughed. "We can say the same, all of us who were human. It was beautiful in its way."

"The thing is," Elodie said, "I have spent several eras fretting, constantly second-guessing myself and my choices, excoriating myself over your death. But now I see that it couldn't have been different. If you hadn't died, there would have been no *deus*. If I hadn't suffered that guilt, I wouldn't have convinced Coby to sacrifice himself, and there would be no new universe. In that sense, my imperfect life *was* perfect. It was the life God planned for me."

She felt Markus caressing her. "You speak as though it's over."

Elodie smiled. She didn't need to explain what she really felt—that it *was* over, in a sense, because she would never again be constrained by the illusion of individual consciousness. She was connected to everything, and it felt a lot like bliss.

"My darling," she said, "it's just begun."